MELODY *of* YOUR HEART

Stories of Love, Loss and Soulmates

Renley N. Chu & Tiffany Chu

Printed in the United States of America

Cover design © Richard Ljoenes

ISBN: 978-1-7377727-0-5 (paperback)

ISBN: 978-1-7377727-3-6 (hardcover)

ISBN: 978-1-7377727-4-3 (ebook)

For Renley Chu,
my Kochan,
my 知己.
You are mine and I am yours,

forever.

May this honor your memory and make you smile from heaven.

Contents

Introduction

The concept for this anthology was conceived between us as a means to channel our experiences with love and grief. While each story can be read on its own without context, a single string runs through all of them that deals with different kinds of love, which, for one reason or another, breaks apart. However, there are tales in this collection that offer some redemption in the midst of loss, and these we hope thread a skein of meaning and hope across an otherwise bleak canvas. Because in a world of billions, against all odds, we found each other and knew in a moment that our souls were one.

Once there was a boy and a girl who met when the leaves were just beginning to fall.

He, a boy with broken wings whose heart could carry the world. She, a girl who didn't realize there was room enough in hers to hold him.

Distance is merely a number to those whose spirits cross oceans to intertwine with one another.

So it was with them.

Their voices made their way through armory of stone to whisper gentleness to soothe secret bruises. And as the days blended, one into another, they found a refuge in each other.

Though the outside world clamored, and inside it crumbed into chaos, still they remained.

"Don't let me go," they would say to each other.

"I won't. I won't."

And they were okay. Because they had each other.

"Who am I to you?"

"You're the one who knows the melody of my heart."

Editor's Dedication

Forever my Kochan, my beloved, my darkling, my 知己, my everything, my soul,

We always said there are no words adequate enough to describe who we are to each other, though we always tried anyway. And I know I will fail, as usual, but I'll still try.

You once sent me a quote that said,

"There's a Japanese phrase that I like: koi no yokan. It doesn't mean love at first sight. It's closer to love at second sight. It's the feeling when you meet someone that you're going to fall in love with them. Maybe you don't love them right away, but it's inevitable that you will." //Nicola Yoon

It seems somehow, we both always knew we were meant to be, though it took us some time to admit that to each other. It seemed that our meeting was a burst of starlight on the black canvas of our lives, a collision of fate, and of souls, and of everything and everything.

Perhaps we didn't know it then, but we needed each other.

And we certainly didn't know it then, but we also saved each other.

There's a strange, inexplicable connection we have, an inexplicable similarity in our experiences, thoughts, and how we view the world. I have marveled more than once at how we were brought together, how I could have spoken understanding and hope into your soul because of what we have shared. How incredibly in sync we always are with each other. It seems impossible, impossible that two people could have a connection like ours, yet so we did.

My darkling, it didn't take long for us to realize what we have is special—so special that neither of us seemed to be able or willing to share much of each other to anyone else; perhaps we feared that giving a name to what we were might break the magic of it.

But slowly we did, and it didn't shatter. We reached across countries and oceans, intertwining our hearts and souls until they became one. Or maybe we were always one, and it just took a bit of time to realize it ourselves. Gradually others began to notice, but still no one truly knows fully how together we are, as two ropes might braid over one another and solidify into one cord of unbreakable steel.

The hours we spent together, day after day, endlessly connected, until we became like air to each other as we helped each other breathe.

Life has been so unkind to us. We both know it wasn't fair. And many times, we've had to convince the other, "Don't let go. Don't let go," until it became our refrain.

"Don't let go. Don't let me go."

"I won't. I won't."

My beloved, we gave each other purpose, a reason to fight for life. Because as long as we knew the other was there, that knowledge was enough to give us something to cling onto amidst all the pain of living. Because as long as the other was there, we knew there was something greater than us to fight for. You held my breath, and I held yours, you once said.

My Kochan, no one will ever know how deeply I love you or how deeply you love me. There is no vocabulary rich enough for what we are. We ourselves were never able to put it into words, and we call ourselves writers. The best we could say was that we are each other's 知己. We are each other's very soul.

You have said no one has seen you the way I see you; no one knows you the way I know you. It became such that even through the limitations of text and distance, we could know what the other was about to say before they said it, sense each other—our moods, our thoughts, things that lay secret and unspoken, the dark corners of our souls that we were afraid of ourselves. We saw it all, knew it all, and we loved each other even more.

My everything, you are the purest, kindest soul I have ever encountered. In spite of all life has put you through, you rise above the dark and give so freely of yourself to others, to me. It is the greatest privilege of my life to know you and for you to call me yours, as you are also mine. From the beginning, I have said you are incredible, so incredible. You rose from brokenness and ashes with your soul intact, and all the horror you have seen and experienced has never darkened your brilliant light.

The world is utterly unworthy of you.

It has never deserved you, but for eighteen years, it held you in it, and you shine, my darkling, you shine so, so brightly. You always will.

You never could see fully what I see in you, but I think you caught a glimpse of it, because you are so secure in my love for you. Some hidden part must have known you are worthy of such love. And you, my beloved, you have, and will always be, worthy. You will always be beautiful, so beautiful to me, in every way a person can be.

You said I was impossible because you couldn't understand how I could see all of you and still stay. You always asked me why I love you, and I could only say that I simply do; there has never been a reason, and there never needed to be one. I love you for yourself: — nothing more and nothing less.

We promised each other we would be together and that you would come home to me, but heaven had other plans, and the hope we clung to for so long will now never come to fruition. And I must try to live on without you, for you. But how am I to live without my soul?

On that last day, when you knew it was ending, through the nightmare of knowing we would soon be parted, still I am grateful, grateful I was there with you until your very last breath, grateful you knew to the end that with me you were safe, that you were loved, grateful to have been with you to the last beat of your heart.

In the last months, as our hope kept delaying, as it ebbed to and fro, we began saying something new. Because by then we knew we would never let go as long as the other was still there. Because we each made life worth living for the other. And it became a phrase that became our new refrain whenever we were losing hope, or when our vision was blurring—over and over we said it to one another, daily, endlessly, and it is what we said to each other again and again, even on that last day. Because this love is ours only, and we are each other's.

"Tell me again what you know is true."

"I am yours and you are mine."

"You are mine and I am yours."

"I am yours and you are mine."

"You are mine and I am yours."

"Forever."

"Forever."

"Forever."

"Forever."

"Forever."

My Kochan, my 知己, I love you so much, so much. And though such words still fall so, so short of what I feel for you, I say again that I love you, and I love you forever.

I miss you so much.

"A love that would change the constellations and the reality of existence," you once wrote of us. And so it has, my Kochan. So it has. For us.

Forever your Roo, your safe place, your home,
your 知己, your fairy, your everything, your soul

About the Authors

Tiffany Chu—

Tiffany is an avid lover of J.R.R. Tolkien and classic literature. She enjoys chocolate chip cookies made by her honey and would love to own a little cabin in the forest someday (where no one can find her). Tiffany lives with her husband and child in San Diego, where they both grew up.

Though their adoption of Renley was never finalized, they consider him their own, and honor his memory by bringing his words to the world.

Tiffany and Ren found each other in the summer of 2020. They will forever be soulmates.

Renley Chu—

Born in England as Leonel M. M. Santiago on May 14, 2003, Renley lost both his parents in a fire that permanently damaged his vocal cords and lungs at the age of five in October 2008, leaving him unable to speak. He became Justin Steele at the age of eight when adopted into the Steele family, a place in which he endured unspeakable horrors.

Midway through 2020, Ren began writing intensively, continuing until his death. Each piece he wrote exudes the rawness and authenticity of his heart, his emotions, his experiences.

At the beginning of 2021, even as his health rapidly deteriorated, we began making plans for Ren to become our family and bring him to the United States. On May 18, 2021, he changed his legal name to Renley Nicolas Chu.

About a week after his eighteenth birthday, Renley succumbed to his poor health and passed away on May 25, 2021. It was three days before he would have come home. He called me from the hospital when he knew he was passing, and we stayed on call together for his last hours until the last beat of his heart.

Though we were never to be physically together, our hearts were connected in such a way that transcended distance, even fate. He died knowing he was deeply loved and wanted, that there was finally a place and people to which he belonged. He died happy and at peace.

Renley's last wish to come home was fulfilled on June 1, when his ashes were brought to San Diego and scattered at Los Penasquitos Canyon.

Despite the suffering he endured throughout his short life, Ren never lost his remarkable purity of heart. He always treated each person as a beautiful, worthy individual, deserving of his attention and care. Regardless of how he was feeling, regardless of his own struggles, he did all in his power to make each person's life better. In the short time he was here, he imprinted himself onto the hearts of countless people, whether they knew him well or not. He is remembered as one of the most compassionate people one would ever have the privilege of coming across. Though he had seen so much more of the evil in humanity than most people will ever encounter in their entire lives, he retained a loving, kind heart, devoid of any lasting bitterness, giving freely to all.

He had no voice to speak with, yet here his words will live on forever and leave his mark upon the world. He had no voice, but through his writing, the world will finally hear him as he deserved to be heard.

I love you so much forever, my Kochan.

Tiffany Chu (Arwen)
Your Roo, always, only

Renley Nicolas Chu
(May 14, 2003-May 25, 2021)
The world was not worthy of you

Glass Bottle

The storms had not yet ceased completely, but the fast-blowing winds had stilled, letting the rain pour down perpendicular to the horizon. It was enough for him to leave the cockpit while the ship stood steady in the middle of light rain, if only just for a second, to determine what direction to set his sails.

Roaming the deck outside, the weather still somber but quiet enough for him to pause, he looked to the north and the south, and he glanced to the east with discomfort as all that stretched before him were deep, dark oceans and solemn, weeping skies.

To the distant west, however, lay an island too far away. Its sand shimmered, and wisps of green and brown peeked out, catching his interest.

For a while, just long enough for the moon to fill up at least once, he wondered whether the island would be empty of creatures that might maul him.

His thoughts, a bit cautiously but mostly a bit naively, poured out just as the rain did, and he tried to keep them as simple as he possibly could.

Until his eyes landed on the bottle. The waters scared him; he'd only ever seen storms as he tried to build his ship strong to sail smoothly. So this clean bottle in the middle of the ocean's emptiness piqued his interest.

He let down a net and caught hold of it, opening the bottle to find a small letter.

The letter, from her—you'll know who she is soon enough—said how beautiful his ship looked from the island. It was so small, seemingly insignificant, but it made him feel real. As if he existed outside the vortex of endless waves in order to find the right island.

Without much thought, he sent a letter back.

There was so much distance between the land and the ship that one would think it impossible for the bottle to always reach the ship or land safely on the island without getting lost.

But it always reached the right destination. Always.

And they thought it was a miracle that the waters made sure they'd keep communicating, or even that the bottle had found the ship safely the first round.

It was a miracle, but a miracle that saved them.

They spoke to each other, steadily more and more comfortably. The ship stood still.

At first it was merely sometimes when he'd change his ship, add a sculpture carved of wood once or twice, sculpting the storms he'd seen. And then he started to respond to her with his thoughts on the growing beauty of the island each day.

Eventually they talked of his storms and hers. She had once been adamant that she'd remain a mystery for their small journey. He didn't mind; he hadn't thought their journey was small to begin with.

Each day he grew reluctant as he thought about sailing back to the storms in the east, afraid his ship might fail to hold when the winter came.

Eventually he stayed, and turned his ship to stand still, facing west. She had been quite surprised, especially since he had said he wouldn't want her on the boat, or that even if she came aboard, he wouldn't be there anymore, for he'd be gone, having become one with the skies.

But for her he stayed.

They continued talking, and she sometimes told him of how, although the island is mostly nice and whole, she still felt stuck in storms she herself had witnessed. He told her of how the wind had started blowing again, but that he'd try to steer his ship safely to the island despite the brewing storm.

A sculpture or two has fallen since then, destroyed by new storms, and the island has lost a few greens too. They tell each other of them while they prepare to meet. They will keep each other going until they do. Every day, as storms recede and then are dredged back up.

They talk, and become constants, holding each other.

They speak of being together, and how she'd welcome him to her home once he was free of the storms, and how she'd welcome him to know the people on her island. She speaks of making sure the island would be safe and steady for him.

She speaks of how, despite her own storms that reach the island, she won't let go. And he tells her that despite the storm at sea, he'll make it safely to her island and hold on just as tightly.

There's so much more to the story, so much, so much more. And if only you could put its beauty down into words, maybe its reality would change the constellations and alter existence with their love. But it's still going; it still has a lot to see and live together.

And they promise to make sure the story keeps going for as long as it can. For as long as they can make it. And they promise to help each other make it as well.

They'll make it. They'll make it. And the story will grow much longer and lighter. And they'll be together. They'll be together.

And they'll help the storms recede and the rain to stop, and the sun will shine bright, and the winds will be of relief and safety and love.

Walls

They know what we've done, but somehow, I'm the only convict.

I don't know who to blame. You're standing there in utter terror as they cuff me and take me in; Mark's a few paces behind, just as stunned.

I know it's not my fault, and it doesn't seem yours or Mark's fault either.

I try searching for someone to blame, but the fast-paced events and walls stop me.

They're just walls.

That's what you say every time.

"It's just walls; we'll make it work." Your voice is insistent, and your smile is breaking, but the nod following each word makes me believe it too.

We'll make it.

You're humming; your voice is sweet and beautiful.

"Sal?" I ask, and you stop.

"Yes?"

"You can let me go."

I can hear your sharp intake and regret asking this of you. But I can feel it: my existence has already started to wrap up and leave people's memories.

I can feel myself being forgotten slowly.

"How can you say that? They're just walls." Your voice is firm.

I chuckle because we both know that walls mean a lot more than just that.

"You'll get caught," I say. It's been weeks and I can tell you're already forgetting me, us, from the edges.

I wish you'd just walk away. And I wish you'd stay and that each second would last hours.

"I won't. I won't." Your voice is unsure, and I can tell that this slow-paced parting is painful, but letting you go completely is so much more terrifying.

"Smile. We'll get you out," you say one day.

I smile. You can't see it but I'm smiling. The walls won't let me see your beautiful hair and soft eyes.

"If it matters to you," I reply, "I'm smiling."

I don't think I smile again.

•———— · ( ) · ————•

I can hear you bringing Mark in.

"Mark, you remember Agosto, right?"

My breathing quickens; does he remember? It's been months, and this solitary living is getting to me.

I can feel my essence seeping into these walls, and I can feel everyone I know slowly forget me.

"Agosto?" Mark's voice is questioning, and I can picture you biting your lip and little tendrils of fear creeping into your veins.

"Yes, you remember, right?" Your voice is unsure, still trying to hold on desperately, but I can tell: I'm disappearing. "He's behind the wall."

•———— · ( ) · ————•

They're just walls, we say.

"How much longer?" I ask. I haven't talked in a while, and it makes me stumble upon words. Your visits are less frequent, and I'm left wondering.

I know it's only a matter of time before you forget. You've held on for years, and despite me not having changed at all because of these walls, your voice is cracked and your footsteps weary.

"They've found a more viable suspect; the case is reopening." Your voice is purely professional and elderly.

"Okay." And I feel ashamed that I sound the same as I did years ago when I first came in.

"Okay."

I hear the crisp sound of heels hitting against the floor in a slow careful manner.

You've stopped coming. I can only imagine you're no longer here.

I often find myself wondering if you died, having forgotten me like everyone else.

I hear footsteps again, they aren't your steps, or your gait. I can tell.

"Agosto?" It's Mark.

"Mark?" My lonely conscience desperately yearns for this man to know me.

Mark is breathing heavily. I can tell.

He's grown old like everyone else.

"I, uh, I don't remember. But I know."

I don't know what to think. Don't know what to say. "You know?"

And for a while he doesn't respond. "She died with your name on her lips. Not mine."

Everything stops. I knew you were no longer here; I just didn't want to acknowledge it.

I want to tear these walls out and scream. I want to grow old like one should in a span of 30 years and wither away just like you.

Instead, a stray, "Oh," escapes me, and I know Mark doesn't hear.

"It was my fault. I told."

And before I can ask him what he's talking about, he leaves. Heavy, weary footsteps. I can tell he's using a cane for support.

Next week, I'm free.

Mark is dead and his dying letter was a confession, taking responsibility for my crimes.

I'm set free of these walls, but it doesn't feel that way.

No one remembers me, and I can only see the elderly carcasses of everyone I knew slowly die as I remain young.

And I hate the walls. And I hate Mark.

And I hope you're okay, wherever death is.

I've given up.

Nothing feels real, or mine.

And I'm hoping I can get to you when I'm done.

The walls are gone.

But I'm set for an execution.

It doesn't matter because no one else can be forgotten anymore.

I think I've broken the world though. Everyone remembers everything but I don't have anyone to remember me.

This is it. This is goodbye.

They were only walls, some people will say.

But I'm glad they're down.

Only some of us might know this.

But walls aren't just walls anymore.

And I'm glad they've broken the world, if only for the forgotten ones.

Dancing Beneath Rainfall

I wanted to write a song about the rain, but all I could think of was her last November. That day, the rain had fallen swift and heavy. By evening, the heavens had reclaimed every cloud, but the pavement shone as glass under the glow of the streetlamps. She took my hand as the sun sank behind the hills. The air was still damp, so thick it reminded me of the scent of summer nights. She led me under the moonlight and when she said she wanted to dance, I only smiled.

It has been five hundred and seventy-six days since she left, and I still remember the way the droplets shimmered in her hair under starlight as she danced alone to music only she could hear. I wonder now if she had always danced that way, and I had simply failed to notice. I wonder if that was why she decided to leave.

Some memories hurt: a day in September when the sky tore itself apart to mingle its tears with mine, as I searched for something to stitch together the void growing between us. And another day yet earlier, when she cupped my hand in hers, and with my fingers traced the pain she had written upon her skin. I held her then as I held her many times after, as though my arms alone could keep her soul from flying away.

Other memories are gentler: when she sang a song I wrote one winter, her voice a clear ringing in the frosty air. We were at the height of our love affair then. I marveled then that she could be mine, this girl who smelled of summer breeze drifting through leaves and freshly brewed caffeine, this girl whose touch left remnants of starlight upon my skin.

My coffee has cooled. I only drink it now to hold onto a piece of her. Outside the rain has stopped, and my fingers hover over a blank page.

Yesterday someone asked me how songwriting was going, and I could only think of how I see her in every corner, her hands wrapped about her knees. Sunbeams always seemed to rest just so upon her skin, as though they knew she did not belong to this world.

She measured out her life by multiples of 500 milligrams, as I now count mine by bars and measures. I wonder how many more beats I have left.

It has been five hundred and seventy-six days since she left, and still I wish I had danced.

Remember

In the grey twilight I see a figure of beauty walking beneath trees painted gray by starlight. Her steps are light, her movements smooth, as of a quiet rippling beneath water's surface. Mist wraps her in a cloak of stars. At her feet, a carpet of peach blossoms muffles the sound of her approach. It seems to me a dream, her presence here, unlooked for.

Time makes fools of us all.

It tricks the heart, makes it believe it has healed, each year another shroud to cover the break, until one day I realize I have walked many moons without thinking of her.

Yet here she is, and the sight of her lays bare the deception of time, for I am returned to the moment of its breaking.

She awakens memories long dimmed, paints them afresh until they are vibrant before me: of days beneath the sun, of walks together beneath these same trees as she does now alone, of cream and peaches and resting weary feet in the coolness of the water; of first love, shy and flushed with tenderness, and the timidity of a first kiss under falling petals.

They say there is no such thing as love at first sight, but they do not know of what they speak. For when first she crossed my sight, I felt a thing like electricity, and cliche though it may be, I loved her even then.

She draws ever nearer; her feet seem barely to touch the ground. We meet, and I have no words. For what can be said when all has already been said and done a lifetime past?

The day she left, the night was devoid of stars, and when she said she could no longer bear to love me, the blackness seemed to stretch its fingers to wind itself around my heart.

"I will forget you, and all that we shared," she said, "for there is some spell yet in this world that grants this mercy".

"To forget is too cowardly, even for you." My voice was as steel, that she would not perceive the hurt beneath.

She looked at me, and I found that her mind was to me a house of closed doors, and I could no longer read the riddles of her heart.

Now she stands before me, and I cannot but recall that last meeting so long ago. She speaks, asks me if she is intruding, and the rhythm of her voice is as a familiar melody to my ears. I feel a stirring about my chest.

"Forgive me," she says when I do not answer, "I saw the river from a distance, and it seemed to call to me from afar. If I have erred, then I will depart and will not trouble you."

I shake my head. "Do you not know?"

Something ripples across her features. She looks into the distance, and a sadness veils her pale eyes. "I think I do, and then I do not."

I reach to take her hand as I did once long ago, but she draws back as she did then. "Sir, you forget yourself."

This then, is the answer to the riddle: that she has forgotten, while I live on, remembering.

Grief makes fools of us all.

Beneath the light of moon, I care not for the things we said before we parted, nor for the reasons we gave that we could not be together. I know only that for her, our love does not exist, while I must wear away my sorrow in a world where she knows me no longer.

Once, I knew what it was to love another; later did I know what it is to lose. Only now do I know what it is to carry the memories of two alone.

Yet memory is not what the heart desires, and how can love remain when remembrance is lost?

"Perhaps you came once to this place in a dream. Night shifts the thoughts of our hearts, and though you know it not, there is some truth in the unspoken words of our fancy," I say at last.

She smiles, and it seems to me her smile is both relieved and sad. And I think somewhere, she knows something of what she has lost. "Yes, perhaps you are right."

She turns to leave. I wish I could speak, but even had I the ability to grasp the words wrung from my heart, I have no power to turn back the tide. Maybe, I think, if she may find peace in forgetting, then it is better this way. I will bear the burden that she could not, for to me, though remembrance brings its pain, forgetting is inconceivable.

I let her go.

Forgotten

Under skies that bore no sign of fatigued clouds, they promised to return, the edges near the other side of the lake pink, brightly merging into the blue, putting on a show by the parting sun.

They had decided they would venture onto their own paths, and live hundreds of lives between now and then, decided to let the world fill them to the brim with stories of new friends and foes, and stories of heartbreak and deliverance, so they could meet one day and be someone closer to who they wanted to become.

They'd eventually pick a pen and scribble a letter, send it far off, and return to the same spot under the same dim, yellow lamppost whose black grill coiled around the bulb like a dove about to leave its perch, damp concrete blocks below, and settle upon a soaked bench with the prettily colored wood to let out the lives they had lived in absence of each other.

It was mutual, a decision they had both agreed upon.

"It's not right. I don't feel right for us right now. It won't be right." Kyle creased his brows, wondering how any passage of time would change that.

"Kyle," Harold said. "Kyle, I can't right now. I can't."

"I'm not making you," he replied. "I'm not. I said okay."

Harold had looked frustrated; Kyle remembered thinking there was nothing to be frustrated about. He had said okay. He had given Harold his space; he didn't think he was ready, and Kyle had respected that. He did. He did. But Harold could always pick out the unease and fear that lay under his blanket of indifference.

He could still be bitter about it. Bitter about how he wasn't enough security for the other to stay together for. Bitter that they couldn't stick together for each other when they needed each other the most. But he had agreed just as readily as Harold had, because there was no use at all in holding onto someone who had already left.

So they parted ways. And didn't look back.

The first foe Kyle made was Harold himself. It wasn't decided on the spot, of course. He had just found his reserves for love diminishing as the bitterness grew slowly and steadily.

By the end of three months, Harold's absence had crumbled the walls, keeping all of Kyle's resentment inside. And all Kyle had left for his former friend was a deep dislike and a sense of betrayal. He knew he was wrong; he felt that way nonetheless. He couldn't help it. He couldn't. He couldn't.

So what if they'd meet again in the future and reunite when they were ready? So what if waiting for the right circumstance was safer?

He had needed Harold right there and then the most. And now, now it wouldn't matter if Harold came back, if he turned around from the dirt road he'd decided to walk and reach for Kyle where he stood in quicksand to pull him out.

Kyle traveled far from the lamppost and bench and the pink-blue sunsets of their origin to settle near tall buildings that hid the sun and busy roads drowning the songs of the few birds perched on scarce trees.

He let the crowded, cluttered roads and noisy apartment buildings cover up his existence and hide him as he wallowed. For months. He tried remaining consistent; he had to support himself after all.

But for whatever reason, his heart didn't feel like it had any rhythm left to it, and with no rhythm of his own mixing into the rhythm of so many others, he felt excluded. Alien.

It wasn't as though Harold had been all Kyle held dear, yet he felt his absence so strongly, as if everyone he knew and cared for were solid living bodies, while he was a wisp of fog lurking in the cold corners of their lives.

Deader

Shimmering light—that's what he saw all around him—shimmering bright lights that didn't hurt his eyes at all. If anything, the welcoming warmth had him feeling at peace.

This sight helped him through the otherwise state of stasis of what he thought: a dead man walking felt like the air: cold, crisp, and powerful. Not even the aroma of coffee he had in his hand could breach his senses.

He mused about how so many people probably pondered their last few moments, and although he could never be sure, these indeed felt as though they were his.

He thought about leaving behind letters—letters to those he loved, and those he liked, and those he disliked and even hated.

Maybe he'd even write some to the mundane everyday acquaintances, like the barista at his favorite coffee place, or the lady who walked her cute little dogs every evening before the sun set.

Or maybe he'd only write three letters to those he held with the utmost love, respect, and care.

Like Dorothy from the bookstall an hour away from his apartment. The woman always made it her mission to find the most intimidating of books for him to devour.

The talks he had with the woman the age of what his mom would've been were always quite thought-provoking, and her tendency to hide some wise advice in between them always astonished him.

He was grateful to have her. To have her look after him from his unruly teenage years to the man was now.

"Hmm, turned out fine, huh?" she'd tease, shoving a pile of books for him to pick from.

Supposedly it had turned out fine, and from someone else's perspective, perhaps it was fine.

Perhaps it was all good now that the hard part was over. Maybe moving on wasn't as easy. Maybe it all still danced and sang loudly inside his head, halting the progress that was now demanded since everything was okay now.

Maybe that's why his second letter would maybe go to Carter.

The man who had stood beside him when he had thought he wouldn't be able to move from what now befell him. It was, in a way, comforting to know he had a brother through those times.

He remembered working late at night, drafting future projects for him, looking for any sign that things might not fail this time in Carter's demeanor, and how in return Carter would reassure him.

A bit selfish of him, he thought now. But he was glad he didn't have to be the bigger shoulder carrying the weight of it all.

Maybe he was meant to help only, by carrying the failures for them so the business could flourish under Carter's success.

He remembered Carter urging him to take on more important roles. He remembered Carter saying, "I won't be here forever y'know." And he remembered laughing and telling him he would.

Well, Carter was around for forever. And he found it amusing how forever had always been in his hands, how forever always referred to him, and in the end it actually was.

He held the power over forever, however much of a detriment that was; it was up to those around him.

Maybe the third letter would go to all that wasn't but could've been. A letter to circumstance and time. A letter writing down all the things that led him to where he was now, for he couldn't write it to people who had already crossed over.

And that was entirely circumstance's fault.

He also mused how it was slightly unfair that people would think him selfish.

Why would you even write a letter to those you were going to leave behind, after all? To those he was going to cause much grief?

Why would he, if he was selfish?

Maybe he was. But it was fair. It was fair because for dead men walking, the world dies for them before they die for the world.

And that, that was entirely up to the world and how it had all the power to stop this. But it didn't, for they were deader than he felt when he jumped off to join them.

Her Name is Beloved

Tonight was not as others before it.

The streets of the city hummed with the activity of many. Faces blurred like the sea that lay at the border, melding together, blurring at the edges. And mine? Just another, lost in the swarm. The rich bustled past in garbs of silk and velvet, leather boots, toting quality purses—emblems of high status in a city of many. Yet on the same street, an amputee beggar jingled a small bowl of coins in one hand, pulling himself along with the other on a makeshift cart, little more than a wooden slab.

And there she was, yet not as I had seen her last. Changed.

When she was born, the earth loved her. Like the grass that swayed and danced in the wind, so she drew her first breath amidst stalks of green, and no flaw could I discern in her. I held her against my skin and traced the pattern of her veins with my fingertips. Yet others could not see what I saw, and for them she held no glow as I had felt when she grew within me.

I would have suffered no darkness to touch her, but still darkness came and stole her in the night, and they said death had claimed her as she deserved.

"Other children you shall have—children that are whole and without defect," they said to me, as though one life was akin to a pair of worn shoes.

I learned how anguish claws at the heart and casts a grey shroud over all the world. But by the time I knew myself to be deceived, she was gone from my reach. The earth shifted and the sky tore itself apart, and no whisper could tell me where she had gone. I passed then over deep waters and ended my song, but still she tethered me to the earth, and I searched for her in every beggar child that roamed the streets, every maiden whose lips were cut in the shape of a star.

When she grew, fire loved her. In my joy at her finding, she seemed to me the sun itself; a radiance flowed from her head and pooled into a light wherever she set her feet. But a fury knitted itself about her brow, and her rage to the world was like spitting embers, for it had rejected her. When asked her name, she gave the one of the city; with no one to claim her, she knew no other title. With such a name, she heard once, and again, then again, "You are abandoned. You are nothing. You belong to no one."

The ominous voice sounded through her head, draining into her veins, bleeding into her soul—this voice was her childhood companion, and I wept then for the cruelty of the world that could not see the beauty beyond the limits of a body that betrayed her.

Then one day as she made her bed in the streets she knew, someone came and told her of life. Someone told her she was loved. Someone showed her what this love meant. In her world where she had learned that people will always abandon her, someone stayed, and stayed, and stayed. And slowly, slowly, she shed the armor she had built around herself, piece by piece by piece. And I gave her hand to another, though she could not feel it, and for once in many years, my heart eased.

Tonight was not as others before it. Tonight, she knew what it was to be loved by a friend.

When she smiled, the stars loved her. And now when she tells her name, it is no longer the name she had received as an orphan, lost and forgotten. She gives herself a new name. The name she gives herself speaks of grace. The name she gives herself speaks of belonging. It echoes a new voice: one that tells her she is worthy.

When she spoke her name, I loved her. And at last I knew she saw in herself what I had seen from the moment of her waking, that she is Beloved.

Stardust in Your Veins

The stars spoke to me. They trickled along the universe all over our skies, stretching over us, telling me stories of what was, what is, and what always would be. It was strange how the pattern imprinted upon this dark canvas imitated the patterns in my head so much that I understood what they told us. And I understood? Of all that were present, I understood?

They hummed and cast their glow upon our kingdom as though vouching for us. Telling creation that it was our stories up there, not theirs. Not anyone heavenly or hellish whose greatness was etched upon existence; it was ours, and I thought our stories could never go wrong. How could they? The stars vouched for us.

The light was on our side. How could anything ever go wrong?

And so I'd walk along the castle's corridors and look upon all the lucky occupants, all the lucky beings walking in and out, and those who lived in town and those who travelled to visit, and I'd think how pure it was to have the light backing each story, each life, each soul.

If only they'd remain so.

The stars spoke to me. They told me how each possibility would end, and they were almost always right.

That's why when they whispered to me that one night, when the cool air drifted through the castle chasing the heat away, and the lit torches threatened to flicker out from the force of it, and the stars said I wasn't going to make it, I believed them.

Their dusty glitter trail formed fortunes and predictions into the sky, a sky I could read, that I was cursed to read.

Sometimes, sometimes I stayed hidden away in the basements to avoid a glimpse of the night, entertaining my sister and falling asleep in one of many rooms. The avoidance though, the avoidance pulled at my navel to drag me out and look. Read.

And I would read. I would read of possibilities, and pain, and happiness, and the collage of all futures that looked so stunning in their tragic or victorious filters. It would make me cry at times, cry at what loss each brought, and cry from gratitude regardless of the anguish.

When they talked of the seer, of me, walking in my father's footsteps, I knew they prepared for me a magnificent future.

And so I searched those days for the successor to Seren, trying to make out hints of who he might become in every future. For I was on my way to the moon where the elders would bestow upon me the freedom of whatever I'd want in death.

Sometimes, foolishly, I'd look for futures where I might make it, even as they named the disease that flowed through my veins. Still I searched in desperation.

What of Aruna? I'd plead. What of Aruna, whose blood shared with me would show her the magnificence she holds? The gift to one day be an elder on the moon.

When all my searching bore no fruit, I rested my head against the castle's cobblestoned exterior, before heading inside with a gnawing inside me, festering just as the disease did. I'd see myself on the moon soon, and I'd have to leave Aruna behind.

Aruna would say I smelled funny. "Ahsa, you smell like wet dirt." She'd look slightly amused, hiding the churning in her stomach.

"I thought you liked the smell of dirt when it rained," I'd say with some agitation. "Why is that funny? I thought I was pleasing you."

"Because the dirt doesn't smell like Seren. It's white, like the moon," she said, biting her lip.

"And how would you know what moon dirt smells like?" I asked, hiding the gnawing tickling growing in my chest.

"Because you usually smell like stardust runs through your veins, and the opposite can only be moon dirt." Her voice was concerned, yet with the naivete of a child still learning the Greek's mathematics.

"Maybe one day I'll be on the moon, and the stardust is turning to adjust for it," I told her before excusing myself to the skies for another desperate search.

When I thought of the stardust Aruna spoke of, it made me feel helpless. What is stardust, if not a tool to predict with? Maybe I was only meant to serve that purpose and nothing more.

And so with my remaining days, I made it known the disease had wound its way around my lungs to the court, and no medicine from all the five seas could stop that.

I spent my days bedridden with ink and parchment, writing down as many of the best possibilities I thought would help Seren and its people live adequately. I stitched up the parchments and bound the spine, a leather cover to protect it. And I named it the future of stars.

As my breaths shortened toward the very last days, and my fingertips tinted blue, Aruna spent her time beside me.

I'd comb my fingers through her hair and call her the future, because the future was no longer me.

When she asked if I'd gift her my name before I left, I told her to forget me, for even though she was the future of Seren, she was still the star burning bright as the sun first, and so it wouldn't matter by what name she was called.

"Why does stardust run through my veins?" I asked her, because even then, the light of a future elder shone through her as if she was a gateway, and her words fell like the stars only in the vaguest of ways.

A seer could only read the infinite and try. An elder, or elder to be, held much more to be taken seriously.

"Because the future runs within you. Because we'll lose a star when you make your way towards the moon. The adjustments you spoke of will shed away and the stardust will be stronger than ever without the constraint of Seren's limitations," she said with her hand clasped upon mine, while the raspy congestions making vibrations through my chest reverberated through her, promising only fading life.

"When you go, I'll look after Seren. You don't have to worry," she'd say. "You should be free at last. No more crying because of the night."

And sometimes when she thought I was asleep, when I was just too exhausted to keep my eyes open, lips blue and skin cold, she'd shed tears, and I'd want to go back to search for life in the stars.

She'd shed tears and they'd drip onto my fingers. She'd reach with shaking hands to wipe them away and bring the hand close to her gently and sobbing. As if she could cry life into me, cry stardust into my veins.

And when she'd fall asleep crying, I'd take gasping, silent, long breaths because it hurt to cry, and lift heavy hands to wipe the tears from her face. I'd stroke her hair and bring her hand close to my lips and kiss it.

My eyes would search for the window and find the moon, following the emanating glow from it, and plead, "Don't you care? Aruna needs me. She needs me. Don't you care?"

And I'd try not to move my sore muscles too much. I'd turn back to her and get up. Shaking from the nonexistent cold nestled within my bones, I'd shift her into a comfortable position. I'd put the future of stars on her lap, cloaking a blanket over her and moving towards the window.

I'd search in the skies, hands gripped on the high window's base supporting my weak, breathless form, searching yet again, sifting through the same stories, needing the sky to stop the suffocation my end held.

Was I not worthy of having my story etched into the star's magnificence? Was I really so wicked?

And as shooting stars would fall on that thought, I'd see my story fall and die. Eyes trained on my end, spirit already struggling from me to go, receive my blessing from the elders on the moon.

I'd wheeze, trying to catch air and hope not to wake Aruna, mourning her before she mourned me. My last thoughts a prayer to the stars to keep her safe, to keep my little sister from having her story snatched before her time.

The Ones Left Behind

I like to think we tried, even if perhaps it was only out of the abject horror of what it might lead to when the road ended for either of us. I think we tried.

I see you now, and you roam as lost as I am, and you seem as empty as I feel, and I think: what difference did we ever make? I see everyone, and I see how unbothered they seem, and I hear how indifferent everything is. I make out how we might as well be the same person now.

I'd rather you not turn into me. I'd rather you forget. Nothing can stop the process, but I'd rather you be stronger than me.

I see how exhausted you seem, and I'd tell you I feel just as exhausted; I'm drenched and sagging with it, but you won't hear me.

I follow you around now, a shadow you don't really see. I've tried to tell you I'm here. Right here. But you can't grasp it, can't fathom it. I'm gone even if I wander.

So instead, I stand behind you and I follow you around, and I see you make half-hearted exchanges and go through your day as nothing more than a phantom.

I think maybe I hate myself for making you into one, but I might be overstepping. Your sick mother may weigh you down more than my absence ever will. The bills and your siblings' fear probably makes you more afraid than the thought of me gone ever will. I wish there's no piece of me in anything that puts you down now as you go through life.

But the box of two rings in the safe and the stack of signed cards collecting dust on the dining table don't go unnoticed. I see how sometimes at night you go over and sift through the ones I signed, your fingers tracing the black ink, reading the words again. How close I'd come, how close. I wish I'd lasted longer. But you're better off. You are.

I see how sometimes you can't even stand the thought of their existence, yet how impossible it is to throw them out. I see how you slam the dining door shut before your eyes can see them, and how you slide down the door. How you breathe in and breathe out and breathe in and breathe out until it feels as though no air is going in. Until tears pour out.

I wait for you.

Because I can't seem to cross over.

The very thought of experiencing anything away from here, from you, is terrifying. And I wonder whether this is any better, if it's what I wanted when I decided to leave you, and maybe, maybe I knew. Maybe it doesn't seem to matter as much as it should. You'll get better. You will. *This is better.*

Instead, I slide down beside you. And my arms are there. They are; they're just ... useless as ever. Like they've been branded to be. Because did they really ever comfort you, even when they were solid and firm? Not if they ultimately melted away. I wish they had given comfort, but I don't think so.

And I wish there were other ways. But there really weren't. And I hope you know. I hope you come to see, one day.

I see you avoiding the things we loved, and I think, *Maybe it's why people write.* Not to stay alive within countless strangers, but to purge out as much of their heart and mind as they can to leave something behind for those they hold dear. Because memories become painful, and writing seems to console; writing things down might make those memories bittersweet. Or, instead, it might make you visit the beach, and finish reading that book, and let you listen to our songs with another, less painful notion.

Sometimes when you're lost at work, I like to go in our closet, and see how you haven't gotten rid of my clothes. I notice how you wear one of my countless grey shirts underneath your work suit every single day, and I wonder if it helps you get through the day better than I ever did when I was with you.

I think of the possibility of someone else mending your broken heart, and I wish it could've been me who fixed it after breaking you.

Canticle of the Turning

[Geoffrey]

“Nathaniel,” he said softly, “What are you doing?”

Before him stood the one his heart knew, unchanged in appearance, for there was the tall form, there the long silver hair, there the petulant turn of the lips, there the eyes hued of blue as the sky above. And yet, he was not the same. Geoffrey’s eyes discerned a fire knitted about his brow that had before never been. And a sight he thought never to see: Nathaniel’s hand clenched the hilt of a sword pointed toward him, and it seemed to Geoffrey as though it had already plunged into his flesh.

Geoffrey pressed gently against the barrier between their minds, though he now knew it was in vain, and the emptiness he met only struck the blow deeper in his heart. Months had passed without the faintest echo, so tightly had Nathaniel woven the chasm between them.

The dying sun cut deep shadows across the forest floor, here where they had crafted memories of joy and delight in the early days of their youth, now scattered along the wings of time. Treacherous time, deceiving the heart, caused it to pass its days in idleness, never sensing the moments passing through slick fingers as sand.

He cast his mind to the years past, of shared memories, of secret thoughts spoken in the night, of two boys whose feet struck this very ground as they played. Golden leaves drifted from the trees, some catching on their clothes before falling to the ground, and still neither could move. The riddles in Nathaniel's heart were once open to him, and he once could read their meaning in a single glance. Yet now as he looked into Nathaniel's eyes, they seemed to him as closed doors, and the loss struck him such that he felt it as a physical pang in his chest.

Nathaniel did not lower his blade. "And what will you do, dear Geoffrey? If you stand in my way, I will not hesitate to fight you too."

"I do not wish to fight."

The stranger before him laughed, and it was a grim sound, fell and cloaked in iron. "Ever you have been a coward, unwilling to fight even as the world burns around you. How like to your father."

Geoffrey closed his eyes and did not speak, for words turned bitter in his mouth. His hands contracted beside him, and he longed to step forward, to grasp Nathaniel's shoulders, to bring him back, turn him from this dark and murderous path. But still he did not move, and anguish robbed him of speech. Only a weary sigh escaped his lips. Was all then futile? His path had long been laid before him, yet for long it had ceased to be one he could discern clearly. All efforts vain, all deeds forgotten. One, and another, then another had drifted from his grasp, some by his choosing and others without. Invisible coils wrapped themselves about his body. Now no path could he see, only a widening abyss at his feet.

"Take up your sword if you would save him from me, for if you let me through, no mercy will I show him."

Light and shadow flickered across Nathaniel's face with the sun filtering through the leaves, at once familiar, at once unknown. Birds oblivious to the turmoil below set forth their song to welcome the coming of the night.

"Please." When at last he spoke again, his voice issued thin, and it wavered, breaking a little along the words. "Do not do this thing."

Nathaniel gave a loud cry, and his sword came forth. Geoffrey raised his own to meet it in a stroke of instinct, and the clash of their blades sounded to him as a cleaving of the bond they once had shared. Together they stood, connected only by such weapons of death as they held in their hands, all fellowship forsaken, yet Geoffrey saw his face nearer to his own than it had been for many months, but only a deepening emptiness did he feel; a faint softening did he see, yet not enough to turn Nathaniel from his purpose.

"Geoffrey, will you not let me go? You know I bear no grudge against you, and I would not will it for you to be hurt, indeed I do not wish you harm, for you are dear to me."

"As you are to me. Yet he is my father still."

"Then do you leave me no choice?"

Geoffrey cast upon him a look of great sorrow. "You always have a choice, my friend."

Nathaniel's face hardened once more. With his sword, he pushed against Geoffrey so that he stumbled backwards many steps. Geoffrey's arm fell, and his own blade dropped to his side.

They remained still for a moment, a moment in which it seemed to Geoffrey he could discern at the last who he now was to this man who once was his brother. A fleeting image passed over his eyes, of a leaf clinging desperately to the branch of a tree at the eve of the frost. He knew it would fall, indeed, must fall, yet as the wind blew its frightful gale, it seemed unwilling still. He breathed deeply and the air tasted of leaves dampened by the early rain. How fresh and familiar it seemed to him, as it had day upon day, and year upon year, and he thought, *If anything must come to its end, where better to meet it than here?*

Geoffrey's eyes met with Nathaniel's once more, and in that moment wished to cling ever longer to the time that had been theirs, grieving for what they had lost, and for the days to come that would no longer be. A deep weariness had taken hold of him, indeed had laid its hand heavy upon him long before this day, since the moment the deeds of his choosing led him down this road. It had passed, all of what he once loved, from his life, into nothingness. He wished then that he could have left a trace of himself, that all might not fade with the setting sun, yet how could he have the power to change the course of the river, strong as its current flowed? And how could he unravel the shadows in another's heart when he could no longer read the ones in his own?

"For the last time," Nathaniel said, "will you not stand aside?"

Geoffrey breathed in deeply the air of his childhood. His heart tightened within him, but no wavering remained. "I will not."

Nathaniel lifted his sword once more and pointed it toward him. Words remained that Geoffrey longed to speak, words he knew would but fall on deaf ears, and with the bond broken between them, Nathaniel stood across a chasm he could not reach. Desire alone could not force open ears that did not wish to hear, or eyes struck blind by hatred.

Geoffrey mirrored his movements as Nathaniel charged forward, and so again would the blades have crossed, but for that, Geoffrey let his blow swing wide and opened his hand.

[Nathaniel]

My eyes widened as I saw in the last instant, too late, that Geoffrey had let his sword fall from his hand, the silver of the blade reflecting the fading light as it spun to the ground, freeing the path for my own to sink deep into his now unguarded frame. I heard him utter a sharp intake of breath as the sword pierced through skin and flesh. And as my mind struggled to comprehend the unfolding of so horrifying a nightmare, the walls I had raised between us crumbled, and I felt a shaft of burning pain flash across the bond, tearing a cry from my own lips before Geoffrey drew forth a barrier of his own to shield me from his pain.

I froze, my feet refusing to obey my command to lift from the earth. I could not grasp the image before me; it swayed and blurred, like a chimerical phantom that changed shape with each passing moment, and I knew not how to bid it cease.

The sword had slipped through with such ease, dividing muscle and sinew, lacerating life-giving organs. If not for the thick blood coating my blade, dripping onto the earth, I could have closed my eyes to the vision and imagined it had swung awry, had not penetrated the one I least wished to harm. And yet my own hand had delivered the blow, my treacherous hand that rested still on the hilt of the sword.

Through the fog that thickened over my eyes, I saw Geoffrey lift a hand to the blade, and before I could utter a cry, saw him tear it from his body. The barricade he had set between us dimmed the fresh wave of pain, but I beat against it in my mind, begging him to grant me entrance. Crimson droplets splattered across the foot of the oak, adding a deep red to its canvas of yellow and green. Released from the instrument stemming its flow, blood poured forth from the wound in pulsing waves, staining his clothes in shades so dark it appeared to me as ebony, and pooling at his feet.

Geoffrey faltered, his legs weakening beneath him. I felt my grip upon the sword loosen and vaguely heard the weapon clatter to the ground. I willed my legs to move, to carry me to his side. With an effort that felt to me as a wrenching from the depths of my being, I lifted one foot, then the other, and, with each step feeling as though I was wading through a quagmire, drew nearer, nearer. The mere steps between us seemed a yawning gulf.

I caught him even as he fell, and soft brown curls brushed my face as I lowered him, bracing his shoulders against my arm. His breath trembled in ragged gasps, shuddering in violent convulsions through his body.

"No—no, I didn't mean—" I heard my voice as from a distance and brought shaking fingers to the wound, pressing my palm against the source of the stream of blood, as though my hands alone could staunch the flow, yet still it poured forth, its warmth spreading across my skin, soaking into the earth.

Geoffrey cried out at my touch, and the sound tore at my heart. He blinked rapidly, his eyes unfocused, pupils darting backward and forward until they met mine. I had seen his face a thousand times, but in the dying light, the flecks of orange in his eyes seemed to reflect the rays of the setting sun and turn to tongues of flame, like the flare of fading starlight before dissolving into infinite darkness. Desperation mounted within me as my hands fumbled at his wound, for even through the haze I knew that there was too much, too much blood.

"What madness took you?" I cried, and the voice to my ears sounded thin and strained as through a tightly woven net. And still I battered at the barrier of our connection, yet he remained closed to me, and I hated myself for the folly of my choice to shut him out—the time wasted, now precious at the last as it emptied, for words that could now never be spoken.

He opened his mouth, but no words issued forth, only a deep moan. Blood instead rose to his lips, and he choked upon its thickness rising at his throat.

I had never been more afraid.

It consumed my senses and drowned all, tore through my chest and clawed at my heart. All other sound seemed to me muffled, but I heard too sharply each labored breath from the one I held in my arms.

—

A memory stirred, of a time when I was but eleven, and Leo had had me beaten for insolent questions. Rarely had he so forgotten himself, but his patience perhaps had worn thin by my constant querying for the story of my past. I had not yet learned that the reticence of his manner did not disguise a warm spirit as it did Geoffrey's.

I had hidden beneath the bed like a child would, nursing the stinging in my hands, the ache in my limbs. There Geoffrey found me and coaxed me from my refuge. It was an age when we had begun to forsake the easy affection of boyhood. Yet, heartsore and weary, I drew toward him and cloaked myself in the comfort of his presence. Within the shelter of my mind where too dwelt the warmth of his affection, I wept for the answers I could not find, for fragments of memory that slipped through my grasp as water.

Do you remember your mother? I asked him.

He looked at me sorrowful, but did not withhold his heart now as Leo did. *Yes, a little. I remember gentle smiles, the softness of her dress when she held me, the scent of cinnamon in her hair. I remember too the salt of her tears, her wordless mourning. I remember when they told me she would not return, and I did not know then that they meant forever.*

His sadness pierced through my heart, and I wondered if it was harder to bear memories of such grief, or if, like me, it would have been better to remember nothing at all.

"Will it be alright? Tell me it will."

He had folded me into his arms then, and my body softened against his. "It will be alright," he had said. "I am here. I will always be here."

—

The mist before my eyes cleared for an instant as a pair of barren feet appeared before my sight. I raised my head. Saorise stood before me, Aiden beside her, and waves of relief flooded the fear from my body.

I reached a trembling hand to them in a gesture of supplication. "Aiden. Please heal him. You must. Please, Mother. Save him." No other words could I utter but these, and they blurred together like colors of the sky against a dying sun.

Within the shelter of my mind, I felt the barrier falter, and I fled into it, seeking him, reveling in the closeness we had always shared, now free of hindrance once more. I thought to help him bear his hurt a little, but as I reached toward him, there was but a dull, throbbing ache, and instead I sensed in him only fading strength, a draining, devastating weakness. *No.*

I looked to my hands, soaked in Geoffrey's blood, and looked to his face. His eyes had closed, his breath grown faint.

She was silent. A shaft of ice tore through me as my eyes flickered from her stony face to Geoffrey's.

"Aiden please, please help him," I cried.

Aiden turned from me, and I saw regret etched into his face in the flash before he hid it away.

And I knew. My eyes flashed to the woman beside him. "You?" No elf was she. And I remembered the word spoken once, the name others spoke with fear and trembling. *Fae.*

My breath caught in my chest and grew to a firestorm as I drew in heaving breath after breath, a dawning realization crashing over me in a tumult of passion. Rage burned through me. I longed to leap after her, tear at her perfect face of stone until she too knew the pain that now coursed in my veins.

But at such a moment, I heard Geoffrey's voice drifting through our connection, consuming all other thought, and I turned my face from her. *Nathaniel.*

It came as an exhalation, carried upon the breeze, so faint it could have been imagined.

Live well. Be whole.

I railed against him, for no words of farewell did I wish to hear. *Stay with me. I will be better. Please. I cannot be without you. Geoffrey, please.*

Geoffrey's eyes had opened once more, and I drank in the sight of him, afraid—afraid that should I look away, I would never again see in them the quiet love that had carried me through the days of my life, the love upon which I had not known I so deeply relied. And yet in them I saw too a grief and despair that I had not seen before. I wondered then how long he had carried such sorrow in his heart, how long he had waited for me to let down the barriers that he might share his heart. And again I cursed myself for leaving him to carry his burdens alone.

He smiled sadly. *Forgive me,* he whispered.

The words were swathed in a gentle warmth toward me, as a sigh before sleep, and I stretched desperate fingers of my mind toward it, clinging to the presence I knew to be his with so tight a grasp so as to anchor him to this world. A soft wave of comfort fluttered across the bond, then, the connection that had knitted us together from the inception of my memory shattered.

And I was alone.

The ground was strewn with golden leaves, others floating down to join them in the silence of the wood. And as each one fell to the earth with a soft crack in the break, the pool of blood spread across them, painting a crimson glow in the fading light.

A world crashed over my shoulders—a realization that a gasping void now resided where he once did. In the calm about us, an icy crust began to form about my heart. Still, the earth did not move; the sky did not fall. Nothing had changed, and yet everything.

"Please." My voice stumbled along the word, then broke. It lingered in the air above me, a cloud of desperate longing to bring back what had only just been lost, spoken too late, too late. Trembling fingers reached to touch the pale cheek, the warmth already ebbing away. *Come back.* The words seemed to tear across my heart as a strangled cry, and I no longer recognized it as my own.

The ice taking hold in my chest grew to a tempest, clawing its way through the pit of my stomach, into my throat. A thousand words burst in my chest, or was it my heart?—words that could never find their way to my lips, unable to take shape in the chaos of my mind.

And it did not matter now, for the object of their delivery no longer remained in this world to receive them.

Vaguely, I imagined I saw Saorise drawing near, her hand reaching toward me, perhaps to calm the torment of a torn bond, and I felt her touch as a blaze that scorched not my skin, but deeper still.

A monstrous pain swelled in my head, driven as from the roots of my being. I tried to swallow back the storm, and with the movement, I felt the ice break along the crack with a sound like distant thunder. I wondered how such a force within me could have been made audible, until I realized that the voice was my own. I surrendered then to the consuming pain, the torment of a broken bond. It broke over me as a wave of fire. I welcomed it, allowed it to swallow me as it washed away thought, washed away grief, until I floated motionless upon an ever-shrinking hole of emptiness.

How long I lay in such a darkness, I do not know. When the wave passed, I laid Geoffrey's still form upon the ground and lifted my gaze. Saorise was gone from my side once more. Her cloak of twilight blue glimmered under the brilliance of the setting sun, and I saw blood upon her hands that she streaked across the trunk of the ancient oak.

So, she stooped beside me, not to extend some hand of comfort, but to collect the tribute of blood I had unwittingly delivered.

I rose to my feet, stumbled toward her. A ringing filled my ears, and my breath quickened as rage mounted within me. Her figure blurred before my eyes, so possessed was I by the fury at her betrayal, the deception she had woven.

My voice trembled. "Did you know?"

She turned from her task. I looked into her eyes and perceived the return of the softness she had shown me those many months ago, yet she could never again veil the hint of coldness I knew to be there. "Did I know that he would be such a fool as to pave the way to his own destruction? No, I confess that I did not."

"Do not—you dare—speak of him—" The words fell unintelligible from my mouth, so stricken was I with outrage. My feet gained new strength and rushed forward; I did not know what I meant to do—to hurt, to kill?

Aiden stepped forth wordlessly from the shadow of the trees, his hands upraised. How small he was, how foolish to think that he could stop me. Yet even before I reached her, she held up her hand against me, and I staggered back as if from a blow, halted by some obstacle my eyes could not perceive.

She continued on, and her words ran as water released from too long a spell behind high walls. "I deceived you not. For a favor to be won, a sacrifice of equal value must be given. This much is true, and I too am bound by the laws of my people.

"Yet Leo was never to be the object, for too well did I know that you nurtured no great affection for him. How then could he have accomplished our purposes? If deception is to be the accusation against me, let it be said that I only deceived you as to the manner of the sacrifice, for there is no power that lies in blood alone, but from the force sprung from a broken bond. And in all my years upon this earth, I had yet to find one so strong as yours. If not Geoffrey, then you must be the one to fall. Yet for the sake of my love I have for you, never would I have allowed him to overcome you. And with the death of one, I accomplish two purposes, for no greater vengeance could I have wrought upon Leo than the loss of his only remaining child." She fixed her eyes of pale blue on me, and I shuddered under the intensity of her gaze, eyes of frost they were to me, cold and ageless and empty. In them I could find no pity, no trace of the affection of which she spoke. From behind her, I saw a thin light like the glint of a blade begin to shimmer from the heart of the oak.

"A thousand years I have walked this earth, suffered the ignominy of living amongst beings far lesser than I, stood by in helpless silence as a mortal stripped me of what little dignity I had, divested me of my power. I have seen what wickedness lies in the heart of man, how quickly they descend into chaos, their greed, their ceaseless striving for power. Long have I tired of living among them. I have done what I deemed was necessary to return to my own lands, and though I should have wished to spare you this pain, I have not learned to regret my choice."

Saorise came to where I stood motionless, trapped still under her enchantment. "We can now at last return, you and I, for you too are a stranger here. Come, my sons. Take my hand and I will bring you to a land of more worth than this. Come, Alistair."

Her last word fell as lead between us, and in me it drew forth a fresh fury. I beat my hands against the invisible barrier, the force of it reverberating back into my body, but I did not cease. A wildness overtook me, and I knew only a pulsing hatred burning itself through my veins.

Aiden had slipped his hand in hers. I saw him look at her with a question in his gaze, fear in his eyes. I perhaps seemed to him no better than a wild animal, yet still he drew near and laid his hand flat against the shield between us. "Alistair," he began.

Something burst within me and freed my tongue. "My name," I cried, and the words splintered against the force of my voice, "is Nathaniel!"

Again and again I threw myself against the wall, in vain, for it would not yield. Finally, worn from grief and exertion, I sank to my knees, my face to the earth. No tears came even then, but strangled cries wrenched themselves from my chest. My hands clenched and unclenched at the soil of their own will. I lay shaking upon the ground.

Aiden stared at me, and again he turned away.

"Very well," Saorise said, her voice now hardened. "You have made your choice and must live to rue it."

Her grip tightened on Aiden's hand, but he pulled away. There was a flash of her eyes, but he stepped back slowly, uncertainly.

"No," he said.

"What is your meaning?" Saorise asked, her voice frigid, a warning.

"We cannot leave him like this. He is your blood. He is my brother."

Even in the rolling sea of my mind, I looked to him. He had taken another step from her. I saw a trembling in his hands, and his voice quivered, yet he did not waver in his resolve. "We do not abandon our own. You taught me this."

Saorise's face hardened. "So be it. If I must return alone, then I must."

Alone, she approached the oak, still gleaming with an unnatural glow, and as she set her hand upon its trunk, it seemed to draw her into its own, and she vanished from sight.

The wall at last relented.

Aiden stared at the oak, motionless, as though in disbelief that such a mother could so easily cast him aside, perhaps thinking surely, she would return.

Above, the leaves continued to fall silently from branches on which they had lived so brief a season. The song of a nightingale broke through the quiet as light faded utterly to usher in the night. A weariness crept into my limbs, and I could but crawl to where Geoffrey lay. I took his hand in mine, pressed it to my cheek. Its coolness was another stab to my heart; I knew then no hope remained. He was gone and he would not return. My last vision was of Aiden's back silhouetted against the moonlight as darkness engulfed me.

[Elorie]

There was a strange hush over the plain as Elorie arrived through the gates of the estate. She knew not whether Nathaniel had succeeded, nor what sight would greet her eyes when she found him. An urgency pressed her on over the fields to the woods beyond.

The days she had spent with Geoffrey had taught her what to expect, so lovingly had he spoken of his home. She recognized each landmark as though it had long been painted into her mind—the meadow that burst into stalks of flower in spring, now barren in the coolness of autumn, the copse still distant and out of sight, where stood his beloved oak tree and the chapel beside it. A thicket of memory rose around her, weaving a darkness around her heart that she, had she the courage, could have named bitterness. She felt in the chill of the air, and in the breeze that rustled and turned the grass about her feet, that a hollow echo of him lingered. Yet what the heart desires is not the dim outline of memory, but solid, incontrovertible realness. It seemed to her as though his spirit was all around her in this land where he had grown. Her heart ached.

Her going was slow. In the moonless night, she could not but take abundant care lest she stumble. Truly did he speak of the wildness of the land, and her breath quickened as she ascended a low hill. Brambles clung to her stockings and stung her ankles. The air was vibrant with the music of insects now come alive with the setting of the sun.

As she reached the peak, an orange glow seemed to penetrate the darkness and draw her gaze. Willing her sore limbs to quicken, she took step after step in her shuffling gait, no longer able to attend to unseen roots that might halter her advance. A stiffness edged into her legs, but still she did not slow or falter. Had Nathaniel then succeeded? Yet the glow seemed not one of supernatural origin, but instead of ordinary fire. Fire? The thought filled her with a foreboding and urged her onward.

Hours it seemed, before she reached the source of the light, watching as it grew in her sight until she knew it indeed to be blazing fire. The smoke billowed far above the trees, and a gust of wind brought it to where she walked, stinging her eyes and burning her nostrils. It crackled and spit embers as of an angry beast. The blaze was set some distance from the silent oak. She could see the great tree from the corner of her eye.

As she drew near, she discerned that the blaze was no bonfire, set to warm against the cold, but a pyre, already burning low. And beside it, two bent figures, one kneeling with head bowed, the other standing. Both were silent.

The fallen leaves crackled beneath her feet, and the one who stood turned, and she perceived the face of Aiden. Yet so altered was he to her eyes—his youthful visage grim and aged like an older man. He came to her. "It has gone awry," he answered the question in her eyes. "Geoffrey is dead."

Once, when she was young, she had climbed the hawthorn tree against the will of her mother. She wished to see far above what any of her kindred had seen, and heedless of danger had pulled herself upward, branch by branch. She remembered her sister running in anxious circles below, shouting at her to come down. Elorie gave no reply, but as she reached over her head, her hand grasped a splintered branch, her foot slipped, and she fell. Before her mind realized her error, she had struck the earth; the force stole the breath from her lungs, and she lay gasping as her sister ran screaming from her to fetch their mother. For a day she remained in a swoon, and only later did she know that though time would heal the cracked ribs, crippled her leg would forever be. But for long did she recall the swooping sensation as her feet faltered, the plummeting of her stomach and the wind rushing past her ears, the utter helplessness to stop the fall before the shock of hitting the ground drove all reason from her mind.

So it was now, and just as then, she had lost something that would nevermore return.

She spoke, and the words were as ash upon her tongue. "But he was not meant to be here. We knew, we thought he would not be here."

Aiden shook his head. "I know not. Perhaps he discovered our purpose somehow. He came to stop us."

"Where then is Leo?"

"He is not here. We were deceived."

Elorie could not speak. A numbness took her, and she felt only the pulsing of her heart, both distant and too loud. There were no words, no words for a sorrow that had no name great enough to speak of its black stain.

Aiden touched her shoulder, and it was like a sting on naked flesh.

"Please, can you help him?" He gestured to the huddled figure still kneeling motionless on the ground. "He has been like this for hours and I cannot draw him out."

Elorie turned her eyes to him.

He reddened under reproachful gaze but pressed forward. "I fear his spirit will wander the ether if we cannot find a way to return his mind to this world. You alone can reach into his mind and find him."

"I will try." Setting aside her own sorrow, she went to Nathaniel's side. There he lay, his face to the ground, hands crossed over his chest as though to keep his soul from escaping. She touched a hand to his shoulder. "Nathaniel," she whispered.

Still he did not move, but she felt a barely perceptible shudder run through his frame. Never had she thought of him as frail, but now as she looked upon him, he seemed to her a withering leaf just clinging to the branch, about to break and be blown away on a single breath of wind. She feared to lay herself bare to him, feared the weight of his grief that seemed already to press heavy and dark around them. But what choice did she have if she did not wish him to be lost to them?

Sighing heavily, she pulled his arms from his chest—they felt to her as lead, so tightly were they wound—and Aiden helped raise his body so that Elorie's eyes met with his. She was struck then by their emptiness as she looked into them, as of a dimming soul already fading.

She took his hand in hers.

Grief. For a moment she could see nothing but blackness, feel nothing but the crushing weight as of a thousand stones stripping her of breath, nothing but the agony of a hundred chains sawing themselves backward and forward through the whole of her body, lacerating flesh and bone without cease. Yet this was no pain of the body, but of the heart. She walked in an endless night, so deep it penetrated every sense and left her with nothing but its ever-present, ever-piercing shadow. Her eyes could perceive no living thing, and her mind knew only darkness. She could recall no sound of laughter nor light shimmering upon a river. No memory of music or color remained.

She turned her mind and groped through the thick web of agony, aching to brush the shadow aside. Yet ever it remained.

"Nathaniel!" she cried. Her voice fell dead in the stillness. She knew not where he was, where she was, had never experienced such a void when touching another soul.

Yet at her call, a faint shimmer broke through the night, and she ran toward it in a madness of spirit, so desperate was she to clutch at anything that would offer refuge from the void. There she found what she sought: the raw, gaping wound of a freshly shattered bond.

Gently she pressed herself to it, put forth all her strength to soothe the anguish. She brushed aside the torn flesh and sent her own warmth pulsing toward it. "Nathaniel," she said, "come back. It is not yet your time to wander in darkness. Come back." She paused, wondering, then spoke once more. "It is not what Geoffrey wished for you. You know it is not. Please come back."

She knew not how long she struggled. At times it seemed the glow would strengthen, then dim once more. Over and over she called, setting a binding over the wound even as it broke forth once, twice more, weeping with blood.

At last, Elorie drew back. An exhaustion lay heavy upon her, and her face was pale.

"I can do no more than I have done. Whether he will return to us, is in his power alone." As Aiden cast a look of sorrow to her, she smiled wearily. "I think he will awake, unless I have fully failed. We can only wait."

The fire had burned low, and mere embers were left of it. Together they sat, Aiden and Elorie, waiting for a dawn that seemed never to come.

—

A grey tinge had started across the horizon, thin at first, then a cascade of pinks and pale blue joined its palette, and with them, hope for the coming day. Faint though it was, still it had returned to their hearts as a star when clouds have parted, revealing twinkles in the night sky.

Beside them, Nathaniel stirred a little and his eyes opened, and he lifted up his head.

Aiden sprang up and gripped Nathaniel's shoulder, too tightly, it seemed to Elorie, for his knuckles whitened and his breath came quick and heavy.

"Aiden," she warned. "Take care you don't overwhelm him." She herself moved closer so as to look into Nathaniel's eyes and saw with some relief that the emptiness had passed, but still a dullness remained, a dullness laced with pain.

"Al—Nathaniel," Aiden whispered. "Are you alright?"

The object of his query did not at first respond, and Elorie feared he had sunk into his reverie once more, but at last he spoke, and his voice sounded as gravel scraping against the ground. "Geoffrey."

Never before had Elorie heard such pain in a single word, and again she felt Nathaniel's grief as though it were her own, a pit of knives from which there was no escape.

"I'm sorry," she heard Aiden say. "I'm sorry, Nathaniel."

Nathaniel raised his eyes to the boy, then to the hand that still rested upon his shoulder. His eyes misted and he seemed again to bow his head. But suddenly, his body jerked. His hands flailed as he flung Aiden's hand from him and scrambled back, breathing hard.

"Keep away from me!" he said. "You. You who stood there as I begged, I begged you for help. And you stood there and would not look at me, would not save him though it was in your power."

Elorie's face flickered to Aiden's, twisted as with pain, and she saw tears starting in his violet eyes, but she could not will herself to come to his comfort.

"I—I'm sorry," were the only words he seemed able to say. "She forbade it, told me no matter what happened I must hold back my hand. I could not—she promised we would be together, our family, and I only wanted ..." His voice faltered, and he could but stand in silent regret, for what words could be said that could undo what had been done?

Nathaniel turned from him. He wrapped trembling arms about his knees, falling into the same stance he had been in when Elorie first saw him that night. She reached toward him, for what she did not know—to comfort? He drew his hand away and her fingers closed on empty air.

"He's gone," he whispered. "I felt him leave."

Elorie saw him turn his gaze inward and knew what he sought but would never again find. She grasped his arm, that he would not return to the empty state in which she found him. "No, Nathaniel. The pain will lessen in time, I promise, but do not prod at the broken bond and hinder its healing."

He shuddered but returned again from the recesses of his mind, where she knew resided still a raw, open wound where the bond had once been, and she looked on him with pity, for she too had felt the pain of his loss.

"Will you tell me it will be alright?"

Elorie glanced at him in mild surprise. "What?"

"Just say it," he whispered. "Please. Please."

In his eyes, she discerned a look of helpless beseeching, as one of a child grasping at comfort in the terror of night. She knew not what he wanted from her. But he was her friend, and all else faded from her mind. "It will be alright, Nathaniel."

Only then did tears start in his eyes, and he hid his face, and she searched her thoughts for a way to soften his anguish, but he only turned inward to himself, and no touch of comfort would he endure.

[Nathaniel]

We are but insects caught in the nets of those stronger than us. They weave their webs threaded with gold, glimmering and enticing, and I, like a fool, cast my eyes on them and followed after their glow. Yet the paths that had been wrought before me twisted to a riddle I could not discern, and at each turn, I chose ill, until at last, I came to this end and a veil of darkness fell over my eyes, and as I looked to my right and to my left, I saw no figure that I knew of from whom I could receive comfort. All the world changed. My vision dimmed, and it seemed to me that though the forms of the trees I loved remained still, their color had faded, and I did not recognize them.

The one I held most dear was gone. And no magic, no pleading, could return him to this world. Such was the cup my deeds ordained, and thus I must drink of its dregs, bitter though they may be.

Briars of memory formed about me, and for long I walked beneath their shadow. Every leaf seemed to speak to me of him, and echoes of his voice hovered in the air about me until I wished for madness to take me, that I might drift free in a sea of oblivion.

The sea, the sea. I journeyed south in after days, for I could not bear to linger in the places we had shared. Yet no comfort did it bring me. Wherever I went, his absence followed, and with it the knowledge that it was my hand that wrought this loss.

They say time would ease the pain in my mind, as a wound hardens then breaks, leaving only a smooth, white scar in its wake. I do not know if this is true. Some days I probe the place where once I had only to reach and I would find him, and the shock of reaching and coming away empty has not lessened, though the days have grown long.

And he will not return.

Stars

There's a story the stars guard within their bright light, blinding you to its existence far before your time. It strings together the gold and silver to light a vow made for forever, to rot forever.

It starts as the sun sinks, its strings of color dying, giving way for the black to blanket your home.

We were a story, and stories are meant to end just as any other, only this one ended unfulfilled, like many akin to ours.

When the stars birthed our vows to keep your silver tied to my gold, I knew only dread, of treachery woven into the minds of our fellow people, to come.

I knew they'd frown at your pale hands as they held mine, and I knew they'd stone us for my hands holding yours back.

They'd tell us that the stars would never approve of such a bond where you and I could live the way we wanted, to meld together and form the sparks of something that was ours only.

If only we'd been given in ignorance, where love wasn't yet a norm for only black and white, for only man and woman, but for all to share as it was meant to be.

But God, how could God have made you mine, only for us to never stay as we'd like, live as we'd like, and reap from what we'd sown in each other's names?

How could the stars have shown me your silver eyes and your moon-lit smile, only to not make you mine?

My moon, my love, my everything, I have to say goodbye. I have to say goodbye.

I cannot watch anymore as they pelt you with misery and break that smooth skin. I cannot watch as they pull at your silver strands and scratch at your eyes only for having loved me.

I cannot live any longer, knowing we've lost our touch, lost our love to the beasts that come from mankind.

And it ends with a man accepting the treason as his lover leaves him in the suffocating nothing.

The day you left, the day you could bear no more of what it took to be us, you took the rays of light that filtered through my cell. You took away the warm solace of my will and soundness.

I tried sunshine; I tried so hard to understand the oppression only I was given for being the lesser in their eyes, to bear the lesson for both of us. I tried to understand how you could have taken away my light when you knew I was afraid of a world without your glow.

You wrote to me of how we could not be because of who we were. You said yourself that my silver was tied to your gold. Yet you spoke of how your honey eyes and sun kissed skin were never meant to be mine regardless.

My sun, my silver eyes now have black taint under them, and my pale skin is marred with the hate of my existence. My sun, as you ran from who we were meant to be, you left them to tear at my skin, now permanently marked with bitter, silver blood more ferociously.

Your presence that was once a strong enough ray to have stopped them from burning me too much is now gone. Gone with the warm winds and the shining sun. And they destroy me a little more, and just a little less every day for being yours.

Only you've made it so that I can't even tell them you left me, just as they told me you would. That you have scorned me to live every day without the choice of fading as you did, without the relief of having it stop.

I rot a little more as I know we're both lost, lost in the darkness, lost to our touch, our love, our everything.

And I will continue to rot for forever, knowing you left me to them.

The star guarding the tale collapses today. It gives you the story and tells you of the silver man still rotting in a dark cell for a lover who could not bear him.

Born, Bound, Blind

Through friendships, we spark and inspire one another's ambitions.
Happy birthday, my Roo.

Born not to you, nor yours alike, a seldom-seen spirit roams the castle in the dead of night.

Rough, cobblestoned walls and sturdy armored guards did not stop the wild nature of child and spirit from wreaking havoc upon the old castle.

The castle's weary walls laughed at their juvenile antics as the residents watched in confusion as to who the young heir talked to.

Paying no heed to the foolishness and striking it off as the early ages of vast imagination, they let the two be, often happy to let the prince have his fun.

The two in question, however, seemed inseparable and content with their close companionship, looking up to each other as they formulated plans and found escape routes, playing pirate and guarding treasure.

The bond only grew as the prince did and soon had duties of his own to attend to. After a fruitless training session with the knights, or a frustrating night memorizing the important records and mathematics needed for a prince, the spirit would stand beside him, lending his knowledge and helping the otherwise-careless prince.

They remained close as the prince developed day by day, and more and more was put on his young shoulders, the spirit a bystander who watched his friend crumble and rebuild himself into someone entirely different than the prince he had once known.

The spirit often wondered whether it was his own doing that made the prince fall so quickly and rise so coldly. He wondered, if he hadn't distracted the child when he attended dinners with his father, to get a look upon what lay ahead, would the prince have turned out more somber and humbled?

Or maybe it was fated so, for kings have only foes and followers, and a prince is but a chrysalis of what a king becomes. Maybe the spirit was meant to meld back into the crumbling sturdy walls, to remain a hidden joy.

Bound not to you, nor yours alike, a seldom-seen spirit roams the castle at the dead of night.

Seasons passed, and the celebrations once in summer now came in winter, the moon's ever-changing schedule defying that of the normal calendar. The prince grew more away from both who he was and his spirit friend.

Now victorious in his sparring against the noble knights, and fluid with the mannerism of all expectations upon his shoulders, the prince's priorities changed as quickly as the passing time, and the spirit watched as, like autumn leaves, their bond broke and fell apart from fruitless trees.

How in the halls when the moon shone brightest, he'd wander to the prince, now busy with a scroll, how he'd persistently, subtly fly for attention, but was met with the same blind that was given by the rest of the residents in the castle.

How he knew, the prince knew, he was there. He was right there. Yet, his existence remained buried in the noise of the bustle and hustle of reality.

He witnessed now from afar as the prince became king, and like his father, and his father's father before him; he became this persona he himself had once hated. The spirit only shook his head away from the sometime glance that had their eyes meeting on seldom occasions of failure.

Blind not to you, nor yours alike, a seldom-seen spirit roams the castle at the dead of night.

Soon the kingdom grew and prospered, and the once old castle was remodeled to fit the surge in time and evolution. The spirit's pride was now tarnished with the sorrow and anger of being left out. Of missing old weary walls that laughed, and of old armored statues that saluted his presence, that acknowledged him, and the wisdom he gave, for all his existence revolved around was giving and giving, until one day he could maybe pass on, maybe fulfill his purpose on the wastelands of a once lush kingdom.

And so as the king went to his last battle, and the spirit smelled the death off of his former friend's once jolly soul, he remained out of sight and turned a blind eye, for he was not one to stop what was to come. And the little princess in a cradle far from the battlefield only watched as the spirit circled the infant's crib before bowing his goodbye.

He witnessed the king's spirit leave the human flesh, and he witnessed the lost denial and anguish, and anger, and panic that remained. He witnessed the acceptance and he saw how the king came to see him, only for him to turn away as if no one stood in his former friend's place.

Born, bound, and blind not to yours, nor yours alike, a seldom-seen spirit passes on tonight.

The Human Constant Equation

For Arwen, my constant

Often, wandering off and thinking, I ponder what the precise nature that makes us human might be. Not the nature that defines us and differentiates us; rather the sole similarity that makes us who we are as a species.

They said it's our need for validation.

But I'm sure out there, people aren't fixated on that. Some people want to give it to stay on top, others want it to feel important. I suppose that's another spectrum, not the constant in the human existence equation.

Some of them said, it's this inevitable need to know anything and everything.

But I'm sure some people want to just unknow all the things they've come across. I'm sure fixation on knowledge is limited to what is and not what one wants to perceive. And all perseverance is different. Another spectrum. No constant.

Taking into account what makes us human, it ***might*** be a matter of mind and heart, and how the two dominate each other to create a specific person's ratio.

I, for one, thought it didn't bode well to let the ratio become a fixture of who a person was. Perhaps it was because fluctuation and spontaneity existed.

Maybe that's also why I stood outside a house, long since the place I called home, with a cake.

The house wasn't in its pristine condition, the way I imagined from reminiscing on old childhood memories; the door's polishing was scraping off near the hinges, and the smooth metal doorknob seemed rusting and unwelcoming.

I had made a call beforehand, announcing an impromptu visit to maybe see a change in the people who lived inside. Or maybe plant a change in their perspective toward me.

These people remain in neglect of the new beginning humankind had embarked on a decade prior to my visit.

The door was answered after sounds of shuffling and a yell or two from the inside, and as the door opened, my sister stood to greet me, her hands on a now polished and well-kept knob.

"You're here." She spoke, her voice a bit deeper than I remembered from five years ago. "They let you come." She seemed relieved.

"I'm not one to make false calls, Janice. May I come in?" If my tone was bitter, it was right to be.

Evolution came with differences. A divide in those who'd sprouted wings and those who had not.

"Oh, of course, come in." She stood aside to let me in. The hallway was now carpeted and as I took my coat off and hung it, my eyes swept over the peeling paint near the baseboard.

Janice had walked away in a hurry, alerting the others, followed by the whole family coming to greet me.

All from afar, never getting close of course. The family seemed tense, and to an extent, so was I. It was a tense visit. One I'd forced myself to make. Who was I if I didn't act on my beliefs?

I joined my mum, dad, sister, and brother for dinner, eyes looking back to see no paint scraping off near the baseboard. Swallowing, I paid no mind, looking in front of me and smiling as the family conversed and greeted me.

"How's work been?" Dad asked, his eyes watching me as I sat opposite him on the 12-seater table. A table that seemed on the brink of collapsing.

The four legs seemed to wobble and taunt me, and the food smelled rotten. Rotten and sweet. The room's temperature seemed so cold, I regretted not keeping my coat on.

"It's going good," I answered, taking a bite of the browning mash and disgustingly sweet meat. "How's school going for you, Matt? I heard Janice quit skating."

Matt didn't bother answering, his eyes trained on his food as he kept eating, ignoring my existence. Looking back, I remember feeling content at that.

Existing was just me jumping from possibility to possibility after having tarnished previous dreams. It was better to be forgotten entirely than leaving with endless conclusions as to who I was and why. Not even I had bothered finding that.

Like the yearning to fit in here, and with 'my' people, only to find out I belonged to none. 'Cause not everyone sprouted wings that flew; some wings were broken.

Broken but hidden under patterns in this crumbling, appealing facade.

Janice had cast a nervous look at Matt, as if trying to decide which brother she should choose.

"Never mind," I remember saying, taking another fork-full of rotting vegetables.

"Did you find what you were looking for?" Matt's eyes fixed on mine with confidence, envy now gone, and I remember feeling proud of him. "Thought you weren't coming back."

"No, I did not," I answered back. As much as this felt it needed to be said with remorse, I had answered with amusement, challenging Matt to feel satisfied with the answer.

Will was a fickle concept; today, it seemed to be a manipulation of morals, goals, and nature.

I remember Mum casting a nervous glance towards Dad, who seemed just as curious as Matt. Her hands played with the tablecloth, and it seemed as though threads were coming off of the fraying material.

"Or perhaps I did," I continued. "I did, and then I lost it again." Looked back at the tablecloth, this time seeming new and intact.

Matt rolled his eyes and then let out a chuckle at the futility of expecting a normal answer.

Raising a brow at him, I shook my head, looking at my plate and then put the seemingly corroding utensils down on the table.

"Dinner was nice," I said, abruptly getting up. My eyes landed on the barely-eaten plate at my spot, now completely fine and not off in the slightest.

The dichotomy was driving me crazy, as if my own brain was rotting from the inside as my life's string stretched and stretched, holding on by a few stubborn threads.

Mom had looked up at me weirdly. "Done already?" she asked, eyeing my plate.

"Yes, not so hungry." I remember my smile faltering and my heart quenching as she turned away to finish her food, and I walked to the living room.

My stay had a purpose. I was supposed to say goodbye this one final time. But not before I could give all I wanted to these people. Not before I could tell them that I wasn't who they thought. I wasn't in the wrong.

I needed them to know, and I hoped it would be enough.

"When?"

Startled, I turned around to see mum wiping her hands on a cloth.

Looking up, for a second, I thought her skin was all wrinkled and deathly white, her eyes open and glazed, hair gray.

Taking in a shuddering breath and shrugging the image away from the forefront of my mind, I answered, "What?"

I took a set of night clothes from my bag and stared around my old room, which smelled like death. All the boyish trinkets felt haunted and the Styrofoam planets that hung near my table felt like they'd fallen and were rolling towards my feet.

"When do you go?" Her question was said with a sadness, which for a second made me want to leave altogether and let it be.

The bed creaked as I picked the bag, and the dresser shuddered as I placed it on top.

"Soon." My voice was careless, a bit of a tell indicating that something was wrong to all those who cared enough.

Fortunately, or unfortunately, my mum was one of them.

"How?" she asked, now standing right in front of me. Her eyes on my hands and looking back I remember my fingers looking blue and yellow.

But unlike everything else, these ***were*** blue and yellow. Below my shirt, you'd see more blotched-up deteriorating skin.

She stood too close. And although I wasn't contagious, I would've rather seemed fine from afar— figurative, and literally.

"I'm not one of them, Mum." I moved my hands into pockets, hiding the sickly sight away from her.

"You're not one of us either," she answered. I swallowed, looking up at her face again, glad that it didn't look like a corpse.

"I know," I said, "I know."

"But you still love us," she continued. "And even if it doesn't feel like it, we love you too."

Despite being shorter, she ran a hand through my hair, and I wish I had stayed, that I had remained hidden five years ago instead of being eager to be another idiot in a new breed of sheep.

My eyes went to hers and then the navy walls of my room. And it looked like it was snowing. Flakes falling slowly and collecting near the ground, dampening it.

Soon after, she said goodnight. And I hugged her close before telling her the same.

I changed. Moved the nonexistent snow away from my bed, and played down staring at snow falling, snow piling on top of me until I fell asleep, thinking of having a talk like this with the rest of the family as well. To fix this before I went.

I didn't think life would fail me before I could set things right, didn't think I wouldn't wake up.

The human constant is a dynamic of the flaws we have, the flaw circumstance has, and the flaw that mortality introduces.

Together, they make it so, that we might never be able to tie our stories neatly like all those novels we write. How even though we'd like to go light and free of all the misconceptions that might float around our existence, that's inherently impossible.

We aren't book characters who'll receive the heroic end at the last page of our books. We might die heavy with sin and no redemption; we may even go light with no remorse.

But we'll still be flawed, and we'll still love despite those.

No matter how alien the concept seems. We're flawed and we're loved and we're hated. And that's the constant in us.

The Coming of Winter

She is Winter. She knew no other name.

She had seen the coming and going of the ages, seen empires wane before her eyes asothers waxed to take their places.

Year after year, she came upon the frost as the last autumn leaf fell to the earth, bringing with her the first fall of snow. She came with ice riding on a blistering wind, plunging into the narrow-flowing river and banishing memories of springtime as men fled before her.

She did not mind; she embraced the solitude of her season, wrapping loneliness about her as a cloak.

Time was to her as constant as the rhythm of the moon, the tides upon the sea. Its passage mattered little to her.

Until he came.

When first he drew her notice, he was but a thin shadow, one of many passing through the story of the world, a faint mark upon the landscape she had walked for countless eras. But he kept coming back. Daily he walked beneath the snow-laden branches of the trees, spoke to her in soft whispers that grew in strength until his voice was all she could hear in the quiet of the woodland. And she, curious, hesitant, mystified, felt herself captivated.

Before the next waning of the moon, her feet began to follow after his.

In his footsteps, she tasted of heat and beer and the smell of damp leaves just after sunrise. His scent awoke in her distant memories of freshness and youth, of warm sunbeams dancing amidst clouds of dust. Soon, the vague outline of his mark began to take shape in her mind, no longer an imperceptible trace riding along the wind, but imprinted unto the earth, into solid form.

At the ebbing of the frost when she went to her sleep on the eve of Spring, he told her he would await her return when the last autumn leaf fell once more. And she smiled, because she did not believe him.

But return he did.

She learned to know him by sound, by the timbre of his voice and quickening of his breath as he walked beside her. For her, he painted the days of his life into stories of radiant color. He told her of days spent among the sheep of the pasture, of the warmth of their wool; he showed her hands roughened by the labor of drawing the harvest from the earth. He told her how he loved to walk beneath the trees when the sun had yet to rise, and listen to the sounds of the night. Through his stories, she thought she could see the marvel of a tree coming to bloom, hear laughter and gay chatter across a dinner table, and she knew then to love the beauty of a simple life.

One day as the sun sank below the hills, she looked at him with a question on her lips, and he seemed to read the query in her heart. The glow of the fading light hid his face in shadow, yet set ablaze the brown of his eyes so that they appeared as twin tongues of flame.

He answered that he liked the snow that clung to the branches, that he enjoyed the coolness in the air. He said he cherished winter's colors and smells, said he didn't mind the lined, scarred, sometimes frozen earth.

He told her he loved Winter.

"Why?" she asked.

Her eyes searched his for truth and she wanted to believe him, wanted it with the desperation of a blizzard beating upon doorframes, demanding entrance. But for all her years she's known that men loved Summer best. Summer was young, fresh, beautiful, and kept people from counting the days. Summer brought clear skies and long days beneath a smiling sun, and evenings lit with the glow of a thousand fireflies. Winter was older, used, weary.

Winter attracted the curious but only for a moment; once they touched the freezing cold, they retreated into their homes, sheltering at a warm hearth, away from her. Oh, she could find joy, wisdom, even a little beauty in winter, but she had never met another who did.

She told him this.

He stretched his fingers forward and brushed the tips of hers. Never before had she felt the touch of another being. A tremor ran through her fingertips like fire in her veins, tracing the pathways of her lifeblood, consuming her. She wondered how frail mortal bodies could contain it. Afraid, she drew her hand back but felt his fingers lace with hers and hold it fast.

"And yet to me you are beautiful," he said.

A hesitant yet hopeful smile lit her pale face. "I do not even have a name."

"Then I will give you one."

Eirlys, he called her, named for the promise of a flowering love and coming hope. The name spoke of the springtime she had never seen, of the blossoming within her only he could perceive, and she knew then that she loved him also.

So she allowed herself to bask in his affection. She reveled in his love, waited for him at the edge of her riverbank each winter, and for moments felt like she could be Summer.

And each year as the last leaf drifted to meet its brothers carpeting the ground in gold, she met him at the boundary of the forest where she dwelt. She led him to her cherished alcoves beyond the river where no other feet had trodden. For him, she called forth the first snow, bidding them drift gently that their touch might not harm, but enrapture. She spoke to him of the ages she had seen, delighted to see the look of wonder on his face when she told him of distant lands, and promised someday, they would journey there. She learned to know the rhythm of his heart, every callus on his palms, and how it felt to thread her fingers through his.

Together they wove their lives, and for a season she forgot to be lonely. The people rejoiced at the milder frosts, for wind that no longer pierced the bones.

But he was only ever a whisper in the ear of the eternal, dew of the morn doomed to fade at the sun's rising. She watched as the years gathered on his body, first as wrinkles lining his face, then as infirmity weakening his limbs. She knew not why a sorrow began to linger in his gaze as he walked beside her, slower now than before.

"I am sorry for the moments that will not be," he said in answer to the question in her eyes.

"There is time still."

"Yet not enough." He turned his face from her.

She looked at him, and wondered, and did not understand.

One day he did not return, and suddenly she knew the cruelty of time.

In the years after his passing, she walked among the trees and drifted along the riverbank, waiting, waiting in vain, until grief knitted a dark veil before her eyes, and to her all the world was cast into shadow.

Now she walks the woods alone. Every day she wraps herself in memories of Spring, aches for the warmth of Summer, and bears Winter. The world is unchanged. Seasons still come and go. Nations still rise and fall. Yet as the snow piles heavy on the tree branches and blankets the earth in a sheen of white, she realizes to her it will never again be the world she once knew.

She looks in the water and sees her lone reflection, looks down at her hands, and realizes she is Winter. As winter rain streams down her cheeks, she realizes she will never be Summer again.

She is Winter. Of all the seasons, he chose her.

She is Winter. He is gone, and she will never again be anything else.

She is Winter.

Trail of Broken Dreams

Trails of gold, silver, and blue flew up towards the barren night sky, devoid of both moon and stars. Upon closer inspection, you'd see the trails equivalent to a stream of dancing dust glowing brightly.

Every once in a while, the glow would diminish, the colors would fade, and the particles would morph into something trying to free itself from the tiny canisters.

The townspeople called it the release of broken dreams. Children would speculate where the trail led, each child with their own idea, their own world. Teens would set journeys to follow them every fortnight when the trails traveled across the sky.

Such was one small child, curiosity the beacon of her being. Her aspirations were still at the epitome of what was placed for her to grasp by others, and her imagination in the process of thinning and stretching into a thin, barely visible line.

The trail of broken dreams, she thought, ended with nightmares. She'd insist this to the other children around her, tell of the glowing colors of dust, the pied piper that would lead them to a haunted dreamland where all children would be stewed to feed the demons.

As she grew, so did her belief, and as a grown independent being, she too told stories, as all did.

She told of how the release of broken dreams glowed bright with potential and died as the hopes behind them died with failure. Her students were always conflicted.

Wouldn't broken dreams collect and try to make room for redemption? Create this beautiful land where all terrors and lack of motivation were fought with courage and strength unknown in their own world?

She argued that broken dreams were betrayed notions left to die and leave their world, to keep them safe and secure enough to make and build new dreams. How dwelling on the past was futile, and detrimental to the now.

How maybe there wasn't even a land beyond, maybe the dust collected into an orbit around their planet, for nothing can be completely forgotten. And the forgotten was very much alive under the surface to taunt and throw blocks on a path so smoothly layered.

Forbidden

It was wrong. Long before I had even started glancing suggestively at him and he'd reciprocated, he knew, and I knew: we were wrong.

But the roots of taint and sin and all the selfishness in between had us pulling each other closer, tugging and playing with each other's heartstrings in this display of pure comfort, and afterwards, affection. The only right thing, he would say. The only true thing. And I'd like to think so. I'd like to. But I couldn't.

It wouldn't stop me from loving, and it wouldn't stop us from being the best of what life could bring in human form. But it'd linger, the penalty against this atrocity that we were committing. This sin we were entertaining.

Us? "We are a brotherhood," Joseph's voice would echo at the back of my head. Bratva. We were destined to provide for our people by all means necessary and all in Bratva were ours. Despite the brutality. And savagery. Because it was for our own.

Bratva became just a cover for me as I stood beside ***him***, and during protocol briefings, our hands behind our backs, out of view, we would secretly hold each other's calloused fingers, with mirth in our eyes and so much love masked behind contempt and a harsh veil.

"Oh Dimitri." Adrian's voice would be so full of humor, the notes playing from his mouth, dark and doomed. "Oh Dimitri, we are so dead." And he'd laugh and it would tug at my heart and mind and soul, and my body would tingle with apprehension.

"What have we done," I'd laugh with just as much mirth. "Adrian, what have we done to each other?" And I'd laugh louder and louder until the tears would pour out and Adrian would take off the sturdy winter coat he was wearing to put around my frame.

His hand played with my unruly brown curls, his grey eyes on mine. He'd take a deep, deep breath and touch his forehead to mine, and wipe the tears away with his thumb.

"We love each other, and love defies gender." He'd speak gently, his usually stoic persona faded and eyes soft.

And then he'd lean forward, hand tilting my face upward into a chaste small kiss. He'd back away right after, breathe in, and look around.

And we wouldn't know that one time Joseph would see. We wouldn't know that one time, the cold, hard eyes of Adrian's father would watch, betrayed and furious at us for loving each other. For being each other's everything.

When Adrian would be somewhere up away from the land of the living, his body in my room with a single precise shot to his head, no blood whatsoever, I'll fall to my knees near him and place my hands on his cold neck and face.

My hands will shake and maybe my breath will come out in short, heavy gasps, but the rest of me will be still and composed—completely composed. I'll go into this numbed existence for the next five minutes until it all registers, and afterwards I'll wail like a madman.

I'll lean over Adrian's dead body, and I'll whisper to him, hoping desperately to play with his now rhythmless heartstrings, ceaselessly and persistently trying and trying to play a song that I used to know how to play.

"Hey, hey, it's okay," I'll whisper, and my breath will hitch and my heart will thump harder. And I'll wish to anyone who'd listen to give my heart to him and bring him back to life.

"It's okay. It'll be okay. It'll be okay. It'll be okay."

And I'll keep going.

It'll be okay. It'll be okay.

Until it won't be, and the dread will coil around my stomach and move around and around and around until it brings out the most desperate of cries.

"Wake up." And from the vocal grieving, these tears will pour out, and I'll wish desperately for Adrian's fingers to wipe them again, for him to lean forward and tilt my head up and kiss it all away.

"Wake up." And I'll wish his calloused fingers would move and fidget like they used to.

"Please," I'll plead to a God who might not even exist. "Please. Please. Please. Please." And then look again at the dead body on my bed.

Oh God, my bed. How will I sleep here again? I won't. I won't.

"Please, please wake up. Please, Adrian, please."

And afterwards I'll be angry. Angry and scared. Oh so scared. Someone knew I loved another man. And they would slander my name and his. And it would be both terrifying and infuriating.

And I'll examine the forehead wound, eyes misted over and limbs heavy like lead. And I'll recognize the pattern, and my anguish will become tenfold of what it is.

Joseph. Joseph. Joseph.

And it'll feel like five minutes, but I'll remain there with the corpse for hours. And it'll feel numb, and the slightest thought towards the forever ahead without his presence will start the cycle again and again until I'm too tired to cry and too tired to live.

"I had to choose the lesser of two evils, Dimitri. You don't have to do this." Joseph's voice will sound far away and would betray no emotion whatsoever.

This everlasting, numb pain will have me staring down below towards the busy bustling streets, the roads filled with fast moving traffic, and the lights only hues of lines scattered, blurring any view. The wind would be rapid and busy as if running away from all the grief.

"Come forward. Now." I'll hear my voice say. My body poised and unmoving, and my hands outstretched, the gun not wavering in the slightest. "You chose the lesser of two members. You killed one of our own while satiating your own sick opinions."

"Dimitri, think about this, son." Joseph's voice will be desperate only to those close enough to know him, and none of the others will step forward, for no one knows anything but of the death of a brother, not what we'd done, what we were.

Joseph will never expose his son's sin to the open like this, and slowly, he'll move forward. The decision between a bullet and a jump. I know him. He will choose the path that seems his own, though in reality there is no choice. And as I circle to push him on the ledge, he'll grip my forearm as he falls.

And I won't think of anything, for I wouldn't be given the chance, but my heart will sing again as I hear distantly the music from Adrian's soul calling for me somewhere in the white horizon beyond.

And as I fall and the music gets louder, indeed, revenge is a dish best served cold, for no sign of Joseph flying upward comes; instead, he falls and falls and keeps falling, and I couldn't care less.

Beneath the Hawthorn Tree

I remembered him in the flowering of the hawthorn tree that stood beside the path we used to walk near our small village, a witness to all we once said in days gone by, in distant memories faded with the passing of time. The sun had risen and set a few hundred times since. The details that had once surfaced in my mind in vivid color now dimmed and paled.

When we met, the wind adored him. It lifted his dark hair until it looked like ripples upon water under the light of the sun. And I thought I could stay here for an eternity, to learn of him, to run my fingers through the crevices of his spirit until I knew every corner and strand, read the secrets in the turns of his mouth and unravel the locked doors of his mind.

He loved to touch the tips of our fingers together. He said it felt to him like a touching of kindred souls, one that did not need intertwining to know they belonged as one.

But I learned that this to him was a veil, for he could not bear for another to draw near.

When we became lovers, the earth whispered of him. I watched the way his feet would strike the ground as he ran. The dust followed after him, lifting as a cloud until my eyes could no longer perceive the details of him whom I then knew so well: the dark freckles dotting his arms, the single dimple beneath the upward turn of his lips. Yet by then I knew him by the rhythm of his breath, the sound of his voice, deep and unbroken.

He would wave to me as I laughed behind, point to the hawthorn, and say, "Come now, before the last petal falls."

And I would follow.

But always we returned to lie beneath the tree as twilight fell, his arm a pillow against my head, our faces raised to the heavens through the lit branches. When summer drew near, white petals rained upon us as snow. I wished often that the moments would slow, that we might linger there and never part.

"Do you suppose the seers read the future in the stars, truly?" I asked.

He turned to me and traced the line of my jaw with a finger. So light, so light. "Perhaps. Perhaps not. Such things are too lofty for we who till the earth. Survival is all we seek. Yet some are fighting now, fighting for rights even people such as us deserve."

A hardness laced the softness of his words then, though he breathed them as a sigh. I touched my fingertips to his but could not unravel the mysteries hidden behind his eyes.

I gazed into their deep pool that I thought I knew, and a sadness tainted my heart where before there had been only the joy of knowing, of belonging.

"This is enough," I would say.

"Yes."

In the end, the key to all the things he could not say ever eluded my grasp.

I wanted—oh, what did I want? A love that might transcend the daily toil for bread, that lifted my heart from an existence of want, to contentment. I did not fear the downtrodden life I had been given, nor did I fear the silence promised to those of my status.

Mine would never be a story carved into stone or spun into song, remembered through the passing of the ages.

What I feared was the silence of those dearest to me.

When the autumn came, the leaves of our hawthorn turned the color of crimson, such that at dusk it looked as though the setting sun had set it ablaze. I saw rising anger knitted about his brows, a fiery storm that I could not quench with soft words. For I could not change the place we had been allotted, could not give him the freedom for which he yearned.

His was a spirit too high to be chained to the meagre lot we have, as was his misfortune to have been born among the lowly.

Within the palm of his hand, he held catastrophe, though I did not know it then. And when I tucked my hand into his, I did not know that he gave the heart of it to me. I could only look up at him, try to read the storms collected into the downward turn of his lips. By then he had cast his gaze far off, and daily he slipped further from me.

"This is enough," I would say, but he would no longer reply.

I did not yet know he was lost to me even as we spoke.

In three weeks, he had gone.

"I will make for you a better world," he said before he left, "and we will be together at the dawning of a new world."

I grasped his hand, a vain attempt to cling to one I loved and once knew. "Stay," I pleaded.

He did not.

The storm broke upon us soon after. It came on our village with a fury we did not understand.

When it was over, I looked over the landscape of devastation. Where once there were flowering buds of springtime and simple joys, now lay scattered remains of the life I once had. Death, which had before been a distant specter that was to us a quiet slumber, was now a picture of blood and tears. Only a remnant was left to give witness to the generations of ages past.

And never did I hear even a whisper of what had befallen him.

The ground beneath my feet seemed to speak to me of him. I soon found that I liked to walk with feet bare, to feel the earth pressing against my skin as a caress. And the tree, the tree, barren now against the winter sky, beholding the story of our love and its loss.

I remembered him in the flowering of the hawthorn tree. Yet springtime would nevermore hold the same promise of future hope it once did.

For he was gone.

He was gone.

Necessary Deceit

For Marwa, the Fred to my George

Waves. She certainly wished to be more than just a wave to those around, not just this frequent pendulum that went back and forth between those who needed her.

She wanted to need as well. Need openly from those around. Without bringing forth rejection in them.

She wanted to be this sudden epiphany, telling people she existed for more than those around her, for more than those who needed her.

For more than the inconveniences people wanted her to fix.

Walking through life seemed in vain, Charles thought as he saw himself revisit his most precious places.

Like the time his father tried and failed at teaching him how to fix cars. He found himself lost, staring at all the gears and wires, something put together so delicately and roughly to compose a moving vehicle. He didn't seem to have the finesse to take on such intricacy.

Or how he spent most of his childhood warm in the kitchen, helping his mom make cookies and baked goods any kid would die for, how he took for granted the healthy banana bread she'd make to get some fruit into him. How he shrugged off the effort at the time, not knowing it might not last.

He visited the times where he was in school, and how even as kids, the sheer loyalty in friendship was so much safer than those that came to be in the future.

He visited places in his conscience that had him ashamed but grateful, like the time his dad didn't tell his mom about the failed math grade, or about the time he got caught cheating.

And times when his mom didn't tell his dad about the various small complaints from the neighbors that he and his friends were troublemaking. Tales smaller kids looked up upon, tales that he was proud of.

How intricate and feeble it all felt, just as he blew past memories of hard work on dreams that ultimately meant so little.

And then he visited the time he met her and how she knew all of that. Knew all his memories, and all his thoughts, and all of him.

And how it had scared him. And made him feel safe.

He remembered how they both stayed away from each other at first.

And how the staying away made him and her curious, and curious, and curious until they were talking and bickering and fighting and then talking again.

He remembered how soon they began holding hands and how holding hands changed to intimate pecks on the cheek.

How this friendship progressed into something more and she moved in with him.

He remembered. Saw. Visited it all.

Like the time they shared their first kiss, innocent and light on a dock, in the rain.

And he remembered how she refused to get orange bedding because he had no sense of style. Or how she used to say she didn't need him to be there. How she was here because she wanted to be.

And how she did need him in the end. And how he'd given her what she needed again and again even though it meant they were separating.

How her knowledge was needed by all. And how she hated it and asked for space.

How she became paranoid of him needing her just for what she knew.

And he remembered how time and time again, he would remind her otherwise, and how each time took more effort than the last until he ran out of ways.

He remembered how she walked away, and how he couldn't save her anymore. How he wasn't needed anymore.

He remembered how days blurred with alcohol-induced fervors and madness of what is and what is not.

He visited and remembered until he couldn't and after that it was all dark, not white like he'd thought. All dark.

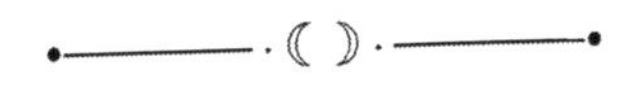

He had always needed to be needed. If one phrase could describe him, it was that; his need to be needed.

And she needed to need.

At the end, although love was there, was it for the need for each other? Maybe both? Maybe one more than the other or the other more than the one.

It was futile to even think as he stared below from somewhere above, her running around and about free.

He turned, thinking he liked it, liked that the dead didn't have to watch over those below.

Angels and Demons

[Angel]

Does heaven sleep? No, but we are perhaps less attuned to the sounds of the night. Then, the demons emerge and whisper devious schemes into sleepy hearts, while the lesser ones rattle the leaves of trees and strike terror into the hearts of children.

And I am the one who lights the forest to banish darkness and comfort the fearful, for I found a strange, haunting beauty in the mourning of the night.

Shadows only take shape within the cages of our minds, after all.

The mortals used to say that the heavenly beings dwelt ever in the light of the morn and did not descend, where lesser forms lived. They watched above with such power as to intervene in the affairs of those below without having to set their pure feet upon the earth.

This is the first lie.

There is no heaven. At least there is no longer, though I suppose the race itself must have come from there. No matter. Its inception is beyond the limits of even my long memory.

They also say that those of heaven do not commune with those other beings—you know the ones—those that rose from the fires of human wickedness to further the reach of chaos and devastation.

That is the second lie.

But mine is not the first story, and I am not the first angel to run afoul of a demon.

Though perhaps I am the first to love one.

At first, I took little notice of him. We are a lofty race, and the demons rarely showed their faces, preferring instead to veil themselves with the dusk.

I knew only that as I lit the branches in my charge, he tarried just behind me, quenching the glow of a light here and there. Not enough to undo all my efforts, but enough to be a nuisance that the perfectionist in me groaned as I retraced my steps to touch the leaves with light once more.

Once or twice every decade, my eyes caught a glimpse of My Shadow, as I came to call him: eyes of dark violet that shone against the shimmer of the trees.

Long-suffering, I thought to myself, on the eve of the second century of this odd exchange. No matter.

[Demon]

There are two kinds of beings that delve enough to think their goals might be met with the copious amounts of gold they wish to be showered with: those who were just hollow fanatics with a dying passion; and the others who'd found themselves thinking more and more of the essence of everything's foundation, the ones serious enough to make it somewhere.

When I was first assigned yet another task, a miracle really, for I had thought the leaves on my tree had all shed and I had no more chances left to stay and be accepted enough to see another day, I had been frustrated. The fire I was made of had bristled for a second, I had not ruined every chance I thought I had to live on.

While a goal had been preassigned to me from the very start, I was not one to dedicate my whole being to its very purpose. I was yes, just a pawn, a gear in the machine that kept the world working. Yet I couldn't care less.

I had a goal of my own, and like a hollow fanatic with a dying passion, it was to see no more.

The darkness I had brought out in the past had haunted me more than any meant to be frightened by it, its ferocity often taunting how I was bound. Bound to this cycle.

Yet when the new task came, and I was to follow a counter from above and undo the light by tainting it with my fear, I thought, I thought I could take no more. The marring of everything bright just by a touch of all inside me seemed a loss. A game I lost to every single time I touched a leaf of hope.

It was not as if I wished to bring the opposite of my being to the world, rather more a need to not be clustered and trapped in the universe forever turning and turning as the other gears on either side of me moved me.

But as he moved before me, casting a sheen of light wherever he touched, I forsook the duties laid upon me and followed at his footsteps.

Centuries passed. Still we exchanged no words, though I thought at times he would turn his face almost to look upon me. We became one, and as a shadow clings to a form, so I clung to his. I memorized the paths he took. I learned to read hesitation in his movements, exasperation under his breath. Yet it seemed he did not wholly despise my presence, and we fell into a familiar dance as the years passed like silver through paned glass.

At last, on the eve of the third century, the silence broke.

"How long, then, will you trail after my steps in silence?"

His voice, low but firm, surprised me. For all the stories of angels' voices to be of tinkling silver, I did not expect it to sound of such earthy realness.

"Who said it was you I follow? Perhaps I have been tasked to counter your efforts in this same country. Your speech is as arrogant as any I might have expected of a citizen of heaven."

He turned then, and I looked upon his visage for the first time.

"So too, it seems, of a demon of hell." And though he spoke his words with some sharpness, I read mirth in the slight turn of his mouth.

The exchange cleaved the silence between us, and ever after, I walked at his side rather than at his back.

Gradually, he spoke to me of things I dared not dream. All my long years I have spent drifting, an existence as inconsequential as the wind that passes through leaves. I floated above the material world, and did not know how to live.

But he spun stories of humanity he has seen, both the evil that clings to hearts as an unshakeable sickness, yet also instances of purity when least expected. He is one who has walked among the people, while I have done little more than pass as a morning mist doomed to fade.

I drank of his words as one dying, though death was a gift reserved for heaven's beloved, and longings I could not name began to linger upon my heart.

"What purpose do we serve but to carry out the commands of those greater than us?" I asked. We had stopped our laboring for a time and sat together beneath the eaves of a tree lit as though from within.

He threaded his fingers through the back of my hair. "We each have our place. Yet in us, I see more of the lesser beings—more human than divine."

"If they carry in them both good and evil, then are they truly the lesser beings?"

"So say the masters we serve." He paused. "But to my eyes, they walk more glorious than we who wander."

I dared to brush a hand across his face. "What makes humans the beloved?"

His voice was a faint whisper as he bent his face near mine. "They love."

And that was the end of words.

How long, I wondered as the dawn broke upon a new day, could we continue? Heaven does not sleep, and would surely put an end to our dalliance. As the years blended one into another as the waves upon the sea, time that I had never before feared seemed an enemy newly formed, and one over which we could not prevail.

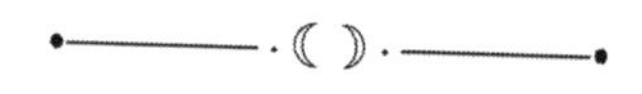

[Angel]

"Why? Why must I choose?"

He smiled, and to me it seemed a smile of regret and sadness. I felt a stirring within my chest.

"Because the laws of the universe forbid it. Because you were born of stars and the dust of heaven. And I? I make my home in the dirt, among the ashes of the earth."

His hand rested upon mine. Only then did I know that I trembled. But his touch unraveled the stirring in my heart until it became an ache.

He turned over my hands to trace his fingers along my palms. "These hands are not mine to hold," he said softly. "They were made to soothe the sorrows of the world and bind the mortal broken. They will sweep the darkness from the land, from the hearts of man."

The truth of his words was to me as a fatal wound.

"One day," he said, "this grief will pass for us both. You will walk beneath the light of the dawn, bringing light wherever you set your feet, even as I set forth my efforts to undo the good. One day we will not weep at the coming of the night. And we will lift our gaze to the distant hills where we whispered of a love we dared not reach for. And the world will shift as we know it will, until the seas have carved away the shores, and the land is no longer the one we once knew."

He laid a hand upon my chest and held my palm against his. I felt the steady beat of his immortal heart and knew that mine pounded to the same melody. "But here—here, nothing will change," and his words were a breath upon my cheek.

I let myself cry then.

Somewhere in the universe, stars were dying and bursting to life, the earth was quaking, and fires were erupting. Our love seemed small compared to our greater callings.

Yet there we stood, together, and I willed the moment not to pass. But time never stills for anyone, not even immortals.

I made my choice. I let him go.

The light of the tree we had dwelt under when we spoke our love into existence dimmed and faded. It was then we learned that in the mortal world, the death of love was a death of goodness and beauty.

[Demon]

He has gone.

I woke one morning to a world still familiar to my eyes, but it was no longer the same world.

And I remembered why. Because the world I had known was now faded as surely as the tides of the sea would wash away all of time, as north would forever run parallel to the south.

I chose him.

Above all other things, though it may have torn the skies apart and damned us both to eternal shadow, I chose him, and with my choosing, I found my life renewed.

Like the shimmering glimmer of the trees he lit each night to shine a light into the dark, so he came. A touch. A word. A glance. I had a sudden vision of a stone thrown into the path of a running creek, that perhaps would not divert the flow, but would surely change it forever.

Such love could not be. We were separated by a gulf farther than distant shores, wider than death from life.

And still we loved.

Even while knowing the scars would carve themselves deeper into us than any wound heaven or hell could deal us. Some stories are spun into myths and crafted into song that the humans pass to each generation. Ours was not such a one. It would fade like the morning vapor, bury itself beneath the earth, long after we parted. Our story would be one of silence, witnessed only by the trees and stones. It has no place among the stars.

But so I forgot my sadness for a time and reached for his hand in the dark.

"If there is life beyond the borders of eternity, will you remember me? Will you carry our love in your memory when all others have forgotten?"

"I will."

I will. For eternity is in the dance of autumn leaves floating to carpet the earth in crimson and gold, in the moments doomed to fade. And we all are but stories in the end. The only witness to our love and its breaking was the blackened tree beneath which we first dreamt of forever, its death visible only to us, though others may wonder at its presence devoid of the light it once bore.

I close my eyes and open them again to a world I must learn anew, without him. I leave behind the longings for who we were, leave behind what we might have been.

Koi No Yokan

Summer had only just relinquished its hold on the days when a voice came drifting across the ocean to whisper words yet unfathomable—a string, tied to a spirit I did not yet know. Without thinking, without considering, I took hold.

His was just another voice spoken among many, a single, gentle wave melding into the sea. Imperfect, fallible, broken, yet reaching towards an impossibility.

But it became more than a voice, more than a wave—an ocean of double meanings and metaphors slipped between each line, an all-consuming fire burning too bright and too fierce, locked away behind glass cages. It was life grasped by the throat, demanding it open its vaults to sprinkle stardust onto a barren earth.

The days gave way to Autumn, and I saw storms collecting upon a virtual brow. I learned to read what lingered unsung in the silences as that sea gave up draughts of rich memory upon the shore, a blend of sorrow and mirth and longing. I thought, *How strange and how beautiful that so small a being could hold so much, so much.*

As Autumn leaves cascaded to the earth, we spoke gentleness to soothe secret bruises and hidden scars, until we found a refuge in each other, and the nights, though full of strange unknowns and unwanted memories still, saw a dim light in the distance.

Winter came, sorrow with it. I thought one or both of us might find more than one scar, trying to keep the jagged edges from scattering into the void. But still we held, held on.

"Don't let me go," he says, and I can do nothing else but cling to his string as tightly as I am able.

I could say a lot of things are beautiful, but for me there's a universe that bursts from his essence, streaming through a mosaic of all he has been, all he is, and all he will be. It spills upon the floor as a sacrifice and spreads streaks of color across the canvas of an eternity. A nothingness that somehow became an everythingness.

It didn't take very long for us to realize that we could no longer imagine a world without the other in it, to realize we no longer wanted such a world.

He entered into mine, imperceptibly, unwelcome even, at first. Yet we were bound by something greater than us, and the string that first drifted over the sea to draw us together wound its way into my heart. It slid past every guard, every barrier, and as my string tightened around his soul, so his intertwined with mine. Through each storm that threatened to submerge us, still the strand binding us together stayed firm. Time laid ever thicker cords upon it, until it become one unbreakable.

Winter storms crashed over us, but we held each other constant above the water. Ours became a shared dream as snowdrops ushered in the advent of spring, as we spoke of being together, until it became a daily refrain.

And though we are less than we dream, too small to hold the hurts of all the world, we are more than emptiness and stolen dreams, more than a series of broken fragments and almosts and what-ifs.

Because courage and strength don't always appear with the visage we imagine them to.

But for each other, we are more than enough, though we may never have the words to express what our friendship means; it is good enough, good enough.

As it is hardly possible to capture starlight in a glass jar, so it is impossible to trap all that he means and is to me within the limited black bars of these letters. Yet here is a clumsy attempt to do so.

Because he sent his string and wrapped it about my heart, I took hold, and though he says I rescued him, his was the hand I grasped in the dark, and I will never let it go.

The spring is coming, and we will be together, and those hopes we buried in our field of dreams will blossom into reality. We will complete the things we told each other we would do, checking off each one and adding to our ever-growing list of things we want to do with each other, and we will be together.

We will be together.

Because I know.

And I love you too.

EPILOGUE

Her. My everything. My soul. I'd write her a letter every day until we meet. From a need to make up for not being with her in all other ways possible. That way we'll create a thousand strands, great and small, that will link us together. Then we'll be so close that it would be impossible for either of us to recreate such closeness with anyone else. And it will seem like we're together until we can be together.

If you imagine our threads woven through each other, the thousand strands braiding into one, then you can imagine when one half of that is ripped forcefully away, that you can probably see the frayed ends. And no matter how you try to bind the edges, to tuck them in, to hide them, anyone looking at that piece of cloth will see and know that something dreadful happened there, that there was a part torn away, that it was once whole and is no longer. That is what we are to each other.

If someone were to ask how, months after I should have ceased, I still continued, why after having suppressed my existence for that very moment, I was still here, I'd have no choice but to visualise a string connected to mine, stronger than all the other, now broken ones. Held together only by her and

me in this tug of war holding each other alive. I feared having to leave before my time, not for me, but for her. The breath of someone I held most dear to me.

My life is like a river current, flowing toward a certain destination. At times, things happen that ebb the flow – perhaps a rock fall, sometimes enough to dam the river for a short while, sometimes a long while. But sooner or later the water cuts through and it goes on. When we met, he became a rockfall, stopping the course of the river, but the water continues, trickles through the cracks, weakens its foundations. Sometimes I think, despite the delays, it'll still keep going toward the same destination.

Wish I was a bigger rock and could stem the flow completely from the other side. While the thought of a waterfall to the afterlife sounds morbid but beautiful, I'd rather she not cross over of her own accord. Want to make sure she doesn't get there with or without me. There are times, where I wish we didn't know each other. Not because I regret this, but maybe because I hold this so dear, and it hurts me when anything hurts her.

I feel like whatever thread is still tethering me to the world is frayed and breaking. If I just let it be, don't try to save myself, surely that wouldn't count against me, would it? But if he's still here, then I have to stay. I have to stay for him.

I wish I could express the visualisation of her my mind conjures. But it's no use. I'd be stuck forever. Sometimes it's like I can hear the last grains of sand dwindling down the bottom half of my hourglass. Can see it so clearly

in my mind, so real and present. Really need her to know, need her to know in words not worth anything more or less or anything than what they are meant to represent; that I love her, I love her more than anyone I have encountered and more than anyone in my life. I wish I could express what I see. I wish I could express what she is to me, but my mind is deteriorating. And words are too limiting. Light has never been so far yet near, and although it is just out of reach, I can make out the direction, and I can sketch out a route, and it's only because of her.

Endlessly connected for so long. Our lives wrapped together as one. I am your soul, you like to say. I am yours and you are mine.

Who am I? I didn't think I would ever find myself. But I know. I'm my fairy's beloved. Never forget. That I am hers and she is mine. I'm hers forever. I'm hers and she's mine. I love her so much so much so much. She knows she knows. I love her love her so much, I can't. I want to make sure she knows even if she already does she's my everything, my everything.

I wanted mornings together, and our hands learning each strand of hair and, sharing the same air, in, out, in, out. I wanted presence, not time waiting for when I can join him. But my fingers can't find his now, though he promised and promised to never let me go. I write him a letter every day, though it feels wrong, wrong, wrong, just like every sentence is only a repeating chorus of muddled memory from a faltering pen. Him. My soul.

ACKNOWLEDGEMENTS:

Michael Chu, my love, my everything, who is the greatest support anyone could ask for, who believes in me more than anyone. I know what love is and how to love because of you. I owe everything to you.

Sarah Fan, with whose encouragement I was able to begin writing again. You are my greatest supporter, cheering me on at every step, believing in me so much I can begin to believe in myself.

Endora Pan, for writing my part of the about the author, and for being one of our biggest fans. Your support kept us going, made us believe we actually sort of knew what we were doing (maybe).

Marwa Farooq, who was our biggest cheerleader, who kept us motivated, who knows the two of us and who we are to each other and loves us more than anyone else. You know we both love you so much, so much. Ebaad Saqib, for your continual support and encouragement throughout the publishing process. We couldn't have done this without you two.

Beta Readers, Ivi Hua, Jesse Wen, for being some of the first to read and provide invaluable feedback, each of you is amazing, and I can't thank you enough.

ARC readers, Ivi Hua, Jesse Wen, Kimberly Chia, Aeval Maurelle, for taking the time to read and review the book, thank you. Jeyran Main of Review Tales, Anthony Avina of Author Anthony Avina Blog, Heidi Wong, thank you for your reviews and input.

Donors, for your financial support to make this dream a reality, O'min Kwon, David Pat, Endora Pan, Tony Wen, Petty Yang, Cam Kuey, Amy Wang, Tina Zhang, Justin and Grace Chang, Jerod Dai, Hannah Tan, Shijun Fang, David Yen, Joanne and Joseph Li, Connie Gong, Josephine and David Cheng, Janelle Ang, Beck Chen, Connie and Timothy Lin, Matthew and Mia Hall, Natalie and Nick Hsieh, Nikki Kumura, James Wen, Tiffanie Chao, Shr-Hau Hung, Linda Velarde, Naixin Zhang, Samantha Chu, Oscar Tsai, Ruthie Caparas.

My editor, Jessica Powers, for your feedback and comments, for honoring the original work and words.

Richard Ljoenes, for your gorgeous cover design.

Natalia Junqueira, for typesetting and designing the book interior.

Made in the USA
Middletown, DE
13 September 2021

47557163R00076